I STOLE MY GENIUS SISTER'S BRAIN

Jo Simmons

illustrated by NATHAN REED

BLOOMSBURY
CHILDREN'S BOOKS

LONDON OXFORD NEW YORK NEW DELHI SYDNEY

BLOOMSBURY CHILDREN'S BOOKS
Bloomsbury Publishing Plc
50 Bedford Square, London WC1B 3DP, UK

BLOOMSBURY, BLOOMSBURY CHILDREN'S BOOKS and the Diana logo
are trademarks of Bloomsbury Publishing Plc

First published in Great Britain in 2020 by Bloomsbury Publishing Plc

A catalogue record for this book is available from the British Library

ISBN: PB: 978-1-5266-1856-6; eBook: 978-1-5266-1855-9

2 4 6 8 10 9 7 5 3 1

Typeset by RefineCatch Limited, Bungay, Suffolk

Printed and bound in Great Britain by CPI Group (UK) Ltd, Croydon CR0 4YY

To find out more about our authors and books visit www.bloomsbury.com and
sign up for our newsletters

CHAPTER ONE

Keith woke to the sound of screaming.

'AAAAAAAAAARRRRRGGGGHHHH!'

It was his sister, Min.

Then more screaming, even closer this time.

'LUCKY SOOOOOCKS!' Min yelled, right in his face.

'Waarrghhh!' Keith screamed back.

Now, even more screaming, coming from downstairs.

Mum.

'Miiiiiiiiiiiiinnnnn! Hurry up! We cannot be late.'

This made Min scream more, standing there, mouth open like a tunnel. Which made Keith scream more, staring at her from his bed, eyes wide.

Then, as quickly as it had started, the screaming stopped.

'Wow, that was intense,' Keith said. 'Remind me what we were screaming about?'

'I've lost my lucky socks, which is a disaster, as it's the final of the under-fourteens chess and Irish dancing competition. I have to win!' Min blurted. 'Quickly, help me look, instead of just lying there like a slug. Is that what you're going to do all day?'

'Maybe,' said Keith.

'Oh, for goodness' sake!' Min shrieked.

'I can't remember the last time I was allowed to just lie in bed. Get up and help me!'

Keith got out of bed, opened a drawer and began lobbing random socks at his sister.

'Are these them? What about these?' he said.

'Get off, you numpty!' Min shouted, throwing socks back at Keith.

'Maybe this pair?' Keith said, hitting Min right in the face.

'You little … '

Min had grabbed a pillow, and was about to bring it down on Keith's head when their mum appeared, waving a pair of green socks with unicorns on.

'Found them, they were under your quantum physics textbook!'

Then she suddenly looked stern.

'Were you two messing around? Min,

there's no time for messing around. Ever. Child geniuses do not mess around. Let's go, go, go. Dad's already in the car. Victory awaits!'

She dashed off down the corridor, then dashed back and popped her head round the door of Keith's room.

'By the way, good morning, Keith. We'll be out until seven p.m. There's some bread in the freezer, I think, for breakfast.'

Then she was gone again. Keith ran after her.

'Wait! Mum! I need to talk to you about the Inventors' Fair in Paris. I've worked out I only need five hundred pounds to go.'

'Not this again, Keith. It's too far away and too expensive,' she said over her shoulder.

'But I could learn so much there. We could all go. A holiday?'

'I've said no once, I'll say it again. No,' said his mum, slamming the front door behind her.

'Bye.'

Keith heard the family car pull away. He went back to bed, where he daydreamed about the Inventors' Fair in Paris, which he wanted to go to more than anything else. All those amazing futuristic inventions. All those brilliant inventors from around the world. Maybe they'd even take a look at some of his gadgets and creations ...

Then he daydreamed about everyone suddenly coming home again right now, saying, 'We changed our minds, let's all spend the day together and have loads of fun, and yes, you can go to the Inventors' Fair, Keith. We'll book the tickets this minute.'

Keith lay in bed a bit longer. Nobody reappeared. He was still alone. This was not the first Saturday that he'd been left behind while his parents and sister, Min, had dashed off early to a competition: ballet or fencing or blindfolded hopscotch or Japanese lute playing or tossing the caber or whatever it was Min got up to. Min was a child genius; gifted and talented. Fine. Keith didn't mind. He had his own interests, such as his Extremely Important Experiments & Inventions.

Keith got out of bed and checked on his latest experiment, investigating if toenails can grow if no longer attached to toes. He had some nail clippings in a glass of water, some in a pot of soil and some stuck into a sausage which, since it was full of protein, he thought was the perfect growing medium.

Before this experiment, there had been the one to discover if worms can swim (they can't).

Or if bananas melt if you put them on the radiator (not exactly).

Or if you can freeze custard (oh yeah).

Keith jotted down his findings in his Extremely Important Experiments & Inventions logbook.

Saturday 7 a.m. – no change.

Then something shiny caught his eye. It was the key to Min's room, lying on his bedroom floor. It must have fallen out of her pocket while she was screaming her head off. Min almost always kept her room locked, whether she was inside it or not. Keith hadn't been in it for over two years. He didn't care. He wasn't that interested in Min's life as a genius, although he did sometimes wonder what she got up to in there. And since he had nothing else to do ...

The key turned lightly in the lock. He pushed the door open and saw ...

'Holy fog!'

Gold, silver, jewels, cups, treasures, trophies, brightly coloured ribbons, gleaming medals – everywhere. Keith's mouth fell open like a trapdoor. Min had won everything. Quizzes, competitions, junior championships, galas, more quizzes.

Keith gazed at the medals and trophies and certificates all over her walls, and on her shelves, and in a little cabinet. In amongst them were motivational messages, in Mum's handwriting.

IT'S NOT THE TAKING PART, IT'S
THE WINNING THAT COUNTS.

SUCCESS TASTES SWEET, BUT MORE SUCCESS
TASTES EVEN MORE SWEET!

IF YOU'RE NOT WINNING, WHAT ARE YOU
DOING WITH YOUR LIFE?

Keith frowned. The only message his mum had ever left him was a scribbled note saying:

DON'T LEAVE WET TOWELS
ON THE FLOOR.

Then Keith spotted the photos. Min receiving her awards with Mum and Dad in the background, grinning. Then – hang on a minute – in some photos, Min was holding a giant cheque!

'Prize money!' Keith spluttered. 'Nobody told me there was prize money.'

Keith sat on Min's bed and thought: Wow! Min's got it good. Not only did she have Mum and Dad driving her to competitions and cheering her on, it now turned out people gave her prizes and money; *actual* money.

Then Keith had a new thought. A new and very powerful thought.

'What if I won a competition? Then I could trouser the prize money, and Bisto! I'm off to the Inventors' Fair in Paris,' he whispered. 'Mum and Dad won't take me, so I'll take myself by winning a giant cheque. All I have to do is be a genius like Min. How hard can it be?'

CHAPTER TWO

'Tom, you know you said I was a genius?'

Keith was on the doorstep of his best friend Tom's house.

'Back when we were planning your birthday. I had some sweet ideas and you said I was a genius.'

'I did say that, yes,' said Tom. 'But I feel like I'm about to regret it.'

'No, you're not,' said Keith. 'Now I need to

be the kind of genius Min is, so I can enter a competition of some sort and win enough money to go to the Inventors' Fair. Did you know she wins prize money?'

'I think she has to work hard for the prizes and money,' Tom said.

'Maybe she does, maybe she doesn't, who cares? I've got a shortcut. You could say it's another genius idea. I'm going to steal my sister's brain.'

'Do what?' said Tom. 'How?'

'One of my Extremely Important Experiments and Inventions. A new one, which I haven't quite thought of yet. But I will. Once I've had something to eat. At Keith Senior's. Bye.'

And he was off.

Keith's grandad was also called Keith – or Keith Senior, just to be clear. All the men in the Keithstofferson family were given the name Keith, even though Keith's mum wanted to pick a new name for her baby boy when he was born.

'Keith is not very inspiring,' she said. 'Look at Minerva – she has become her name, wise and talented, like the Roman goddess of wisdom. There was no Roman god Keith.'

But Keith's dad, Keith, insisted. So did Keith Sr.

'You can't go wrong with the name Keith,' Keith Sr said, bouncing baby Keith on his knee, roughly eleven years ago. 'It's not fancy or flash, but it's solid, with a hint of mischief. I think my best achievements were because of the name Keith. My hit song – "The Keith Is On". My range of sauces called Keith's Condiments. And my personally designed range of spoons, forks and knives, known as Keith's Utterly Cutlery.'

These days, Keith Sr lived on a canal boat named *Drifter*, which was moored up next to a disused soap factory. From his favourite seat on deck, where he was enjoying the warm July sun, he spotted Keith running down the towpath. Peanuts, his cheese-obsessed parrot, saw him, too, and squawked, 'Dairylea!'

'Can I have one of your special crisp sand-wiches?' Keith asked as he hopped aboard. 'I've got some serious inventing to do this afternoon and I need the energy.'

'More inventing? Excellent. What are you making?' Keith Sr asked.

'A machine that can steal Min's brain.'

'Really? Sounds a bit rough for Min,' said Keith Sr.

'It's all right, it won't hurt her,' Keith said.

'Good, but what's wrong with your brain, anyway?' Keith Sr asked. 'You're super smart, in your own unique Keith way. Maybe not book-smart like Min, but you know plenty of interesting things.'

'True, I do. I know ostriches can run faster than horses. I know a tarantula can survive for more than two years without food and alligators can live for a hundred years. Almost as old as you.'

'Watch it,' said Keith Sr.

'I also discovered that heat slows your brain workings down. That's why I invented Keith's Anti-Heat Headgear.'

'Sounds cool,' said Keith Sr.

'It literally is,' said Keith.

'So, why exactly do you want to steal Min's brain?' Keith Sr asked.

'To get all the knowledge in it, so I can win prize money at those genius competitions and quizzes she goes to. Then I can afford to go to the Inventors' Fair in Paris. Mum and Dad won't take me.'

'I'd take you myself,' said Keith Sr, 'but

I'm broke, and I'm not sure *Drifter* could make it over the Channel. But is stealing Min's brain the best way? What about washing people's cars?'

'There's no time. I'd have to wash loads of cars to raise enough and besides, the fair is in three weeks. It has to be an invention. Inventing is what I do best. I've got to try.'

'Well, sure, it's amazing what you can achieve if you try. But before you try, you've got to eat,' said Keith Sr. 'Come on, son, let's make those crisp sandwiches.'

CHAPTER THREE

As soon as Keith got home, he took out his biggest sketch pad and some colourful pens and began sketching ideas for a brain-stealing gadget. Keith liked to make drawings when he was thinking of a new invention. He called it Free Noodling. It was while using his Free Noodling method that he'd invented bread scissors, for slicing bread without the need of a knife, and the head sock, also known as the full balaclava, for complete face warmth.

Keith drew himself, then he drew Min, and then he drew giant arrows between their two heads.

'I need to get her genius ideas over to my brain instantly, like a flash of lightning ... '

He sketched some lightning bolts.

'Or like electricity going along a wire,' he said, and began drawing wires connecting their two heads.

Then he found himself drawing a sort of giant helmet on Min's head, which looked quite a lot like a big sieve.

'That's it!' he shouted, and raced downstairs.

Keith spent the next hour or so attaching wires from his dad's toolbox to the shiny metal sieve from the kitchen which was used to drain pasta. He then found an old metal biscuit tin which fitted snugly on his head. He tinkered with it, piercing holes here, attaching wires there, and then admired his handiwork.

The brain-stealing headset looked properly sciencey – all those wires! – but would it work? He had no one to test it on. He briefly considered calling Tom, but decided there wasn't time. There was, however, just enough time to check on his toenail experiment. Keith examined each toenail and wrote down the findings – **no change**. Then he remembered another experiment that was under way: Extremely Important Experiment Number 37 – Buried Sandwich. He rushed down to the garden and searched beneath a pile of grass clippings. There was nothing there. He wrote down:

Sandwich gone. No sign of a struggle. Site disturbed but no crumbs. Hmmm...

Then he wrote: Fox.

'Definitely a fox. My experiment has successfully proved that foxes like sandwiches. Good.'

His phone rang.

'Hi, Keith,' said a voice.

'Who is this?' Keith said.

'It's Mum!' said his mum. 'We're on our way back. See you in twenty minutes. Min won again. Isn't she amazing?'

'I just discovered that foxes like sandwiches,' said Keith.

'Foxes lick what? You're breaking up, Keith,' said his mum. 'Bye.'

When Min came through the front door she was holding several balloons, saying **WINNER** and **CHAMPION**.

'Hey, are those helium balloons?' Keith asked.

Before Min could reply, he pierced one with his teeth and breathed in the helium.

'Is that a biscuit tin on your head?' said Keith's dad. 'Ridiculous.'

'No, not ridiculous. Crackers, maybe,' said Keith in a voice that was extremely high and squeaky.

The corner of Min's mouth flickered.

'Stop being silly, Keith,' said Keith's mum.

The phone rang.

'And do not answer the phone with that squeaky voice!' she said.

Too late.

'Good evening, Keithstofferson residence, how may I be of assistingance?' Keith squeaked.

Min spluttered a laugh now. Mum snatched the phone.

'I'm so sorry, Mrs Keithstofferson speaking,' she said. 'No, that wasn't a pixie, it was my son. Helium balloons, yes, very amusing. Yes, of course you can interview Min about her latest victory. I'll pass you over.'

She held the phone out to Min.

'It's the local paper. They want an interview.'

'Sure,' said Min, then quickly popped a balloon, breathed it in and grabbed the phone.

'Min speaking,' she said, in a cartoon-mouse voice absolutely squeaking with helium.

Keith roared with laughter, and Min was giggle-squeaking now. Mum grabbed the phone and rushed into the sitting room, apologising.

'That is not the right way to behave when

you've just won the under-fourteens chess and Irish dancing competition,' said Dad.

'Why not?' Keith squeaked. 'It's funny.'

'It's silly. Like that tin on your head,' said Dad.

'Yeah, why *do* you have a biscuit tin on your head, Keith?' Min asked. 'Tell me, I promise I'll understand. I am a genius, after all.'

'So you are,' said Keith. 'Well, if you'll step into my bedroom, I'll explain everything.'

Once upstairs, Keith closed his door.

'I am working on a new costume for Halloween,' he said.

'That's months away,' said Min.

'It's good to be prepared,' said Keith.

'What are you meant to be?' asked Min.

'A sort of mad scientist who is doing things to other people's brains,' said Keith.

'What kind of things?' asked Min.

'Just things, OK? Wow, you ask a lot of questions.'

'I've got an enquiring mind,' said Min. 'All part of being a genius.'

'I've got an enquiring mind, too,' said Keith. 'I just don't want to enquire about the same stuff as you enquire about.'

He plonked the sieve on Min's head.

'Just help me out by wearing this on your head for a moment, please.'

He then quickly attached the wires to the biscuit tin on his own head. Then he grabbed a battery, which he thought would supply some useful extra power, gripped it hard and, standing very close to Min, stared into her eyes and waited for her brain to dart down the wires and into his. Keith had expected a huge jolt of sudden knowledge

to thump into his head, with perhaps some dramatic sparks crackling above, too, but nothing happened.

'Why are you staring at me?' Min asked. 'You look like you've peed yourself but don't want to admit it.'

Keith said nothing.

'Hello, Keith, are you OK?' Min tapped the tin on his head. *Tap, tap, tap!*

Keith carried on staring. Min stared back for one second, two, then ...

'This is the worst Halloween costume I've ever seen and you're being weird,' she said.

She yanked the sieve off and threw it down. It bounced on the wires and pinged back up, like a sieve bungee jumper, and thumped Keith in the face.

'Owww,' he yelled. 'What did you have to sieve me for?'

'Sieves you right,' said Min, and stomped downstairs.

Keith pulled the biscuit tin off his head. He checked to see if he was having any genius thoughts. Nothing.

His phone rang.

'Hi, Keith,' said a voice.

'Who is this?' said Keith.

'It's Tom, your best friend,' said Tom. 'Did you steal your sister's brain yet?'

'Well, I made an amazing brain-stealing headset with a big sieve and wires – loads of wires! – and a biscuit tin and it was very cool and clever.'

'And?' said Tom.

'I don't think it worked,' said Keith. 'But let's check. Ask me something hard.'

'What's the capital of Uzbekistan?'

'Dunno,' said Keith.

'What's the square root of six hundred and twenty-three?' Tom asked.

'No clue,' said Keith. 'As I suspected. It didn't work.'

'I wonder why?' said Tom.

'Maybe the wires were faulty,' said Keith. 'Maybe I don't need wires at all, or a gadget.'

'Or maybe you should give up?' said Tom.

'What? No! Keith never gives up. It's the Keithstofferson spirit. But I may sleep on it. I'm quite tired, actually. Trying to steal someone's brain is harder than I realised.'

CHAPTER FOUR

Keith slept deeply, with no dreams, and woke refreshed. Better than that, he woke with another genius idea of how to steal Min's brain. Hypnosis!

'I'm going to hypnotise my sister,' Keith said to himself. 'Yes! Then, while Min's under my power, she can tell me everything I need to know about being a genius.'

Keith had tried hypnosis once before, on

his neighbour's cat, Chops, using a Party Ring biscuit swinging on a thread. Chops had batted it with his paw, then settled into a hypnotised state (although possibly Chops was just asleep). After that, Keith didn't remember what happened. He had become completely focused on the swinging Party Ring, until Min told him he was back in the room, or something.

This time, Keith decided to do some research. He spent the morning reading all about hypnosis, learning how to put someone into a trance, and then went downstairs for lunch.

Keith ate hurriedly, and then sat waiting for Min to finish so he could begin the hypnosis. There was no time to lose – after all, the Inventors' Fair was in three weeks. This was urgent with a capital Urge.

As soon as Min had put down her knife and fork, Keith pounced.

'You look tired, Min. Why don't you lie on the sofa?'

'What are you doing?' she asked, as he ushered her towards the living room.

'Just being nice to my genius sister, what's wrong with that?' he said. 'Relax. Sink back into the sofa. Everything here is very calm and peaceful.'

'I repeat – what are you doing?' Min asked, as Keith helped her lie back against the cushions.

'Your eyes feel very heavy and want to close, after all the genius work you've been doing. Let your eyes close and your body close and your muscles go soft like warm jelly … '

Keith couldn't remember exactly what he was meant to say, but he was determined to keep the hypnotic mood going.

'Listen to my voice, my voice, my lovely voice, and feel really calm, and relaxed and sleepy and warm and lazy and warm.'

Min said nothing, but her eyes began to close. She's going, thought Keith, I'm doing it.

'You are really sleepy now, so sleepy and heavy, like a tired little chick that's been flapping around all day, or a baby mouse.'

Min yawned.

'You are slipping deeper into a calm state, and feeling very calm. Now you are open to my suggestions,' said Keith. 'You will tell me everything you know about being a genius, because you want to share, share all your knowledge and facts and any good tips. Share, share. This is not stealing, by the way, you're sharing, sharing, sharing ... '

Keith then held his breath, watching his motionless sister.

'Wear yellow pants,' Min muttered. 'And eat only celery the night before a competition.'

Holy bog, Keith thought, I don't think I have any yellow pants and I absolutely hate celery.

'Don't do any studying before a quiz, it's not worth it,' Min mumbled. 'I don't do any work before competitions – I just turn up.'

'I knew it!' Keith said.

'And remember to … ' Min's eyes pinged open and she sat up, grabbed Keith by the shoulders and yelled in his face, 'Stop being such an idiot!'

Keith screamed and sprang away.

'You scared me! Wait, what just happened? Were you in a trance or not?'

'Of course I wasn't, Keith, I'm far too clever

to be hypnotised by you,' Min said. 'I know all about hypnosis. I wasn't going to fall into a trance just because you said I was as tired as a baby chick.'

'You tricked me!' he said.

'Yes, I did. I'm sorry. Come and sit here.' She patted the sofa. 'Now, relax. Let all your weight sink into the cushions.'

Keith sat down heavily.

'I apologise, Keith. That was naughty of me. Relax now. Let your eyes close and breathe deeply,' said Min. Her voice had gone soft and slow.

'You're sinking down and shutting down, sinking down and shutting down,' she said. 'You're slipping into a state of blissful relax-ation. You have floated above your body, far above your body.'

Min softly clicked her fingers in front

of Keith's face. No reaction.

'Why did you try to hypnotise me, Keith?' she asked.

'Want to be a genius,' he mumbled. 'Mum and Dad smiling. Very proud of me. Clapping. Balloons. Giant cheques! Go to the Inventors' Fair.'

Min frowned.

'I'm not sure you do want to be a genius, Keith. It's really hard work,' said Min. 'Mum and Dad are constantly on at me. I have to study and train all day. I don't have any free time like you do.'

Keith mumbled and tossed his head from side to side.

'What was the sieve on my head for?' Min asked.

'Stealing your brain,' he said. 'Steal all the facts.'

Min sighed and shook her head. Then she had an idea:

'Keith, you are now a snake, slithering along the floor.'

Keith threw himself on to the floor and twisted across it on his belly, hissing.

'Now you're a sleepy puppy.'

Keith did an excellent sleepy puppy, yawning and lolloping about. Min felt she could have watched him for hours, but she had algebra homework to do.

'When I count to five you will be fully awake, fully alert and completely refreshed. One, two, three, four, five ... '

Keith's eyes opened.

'I feel great,' he said. 'Did I just nod off?'

'Yeah, something like that,' said Min.

CHAPTER FIVE

Back in his room, Keith pulled out his sketch pad again and grabbed a pen. He needed a new plan for stealing Min's brain. His headset had not worked and neither had hypnosis, but he was sure there had to be another way to harness all Min's brainpower.

'I think I read that brainwaves can actually cross over if you're close enough to the other person's head,' Keith muttered.

'Or did I dream that? Never mind, it's worth a go.'

He sketched himself and Min again, this time with their heads touching and a giant light bulb above his, to show that all the genius wisdom had successfully zipped into it from Min's.

'Perfect,' Keith muttered. 'Now I just need to get closer to Min, in a relaxed way. Let the brainwaves flow across. No wires, no sieves.'

Keith found Min downstairs in the living room, reading a maths textbook.

'I want to apologise for making you wear a sieve yesterday and for trying to hypnotise you earlier,' he said. 'Can I give you a relaxing head massage, to say sorry?'

'Are you still trying to steal my brain?' Min asked.

'Of course not,' said Keith. 'I just want to

help you. Mum and Dad don't understand about the need to unwind, but I really do.'

'That's true. Mum and Dad never give me a break,' Min said.

She sat on the floor and Keith clambered on to the sofa behind her and began rubbing her head.

'Since when did you take an interest in my competitions? Or my health?' said Min, her head bobbing about as Keith rubbed it.

'Shhh, just enjoy the massage,' he said, willing all her genius brainwaves to flow up through his hands and into his brain.

'Ouch,' said Min. Keith's hands snagged in her long hair. He moved his fingers round to her forehead. Surely there was tons of genius info right there, at the front. He dragged them across, making her eyes stretch out weirdly. Then he lightly rippled his fingers across the top of her head, like he was playing the piano.

'That tickles!' Min said. 'OK, that's probably enough head massaging for now, thanks.'

Before she could get up, Keith rubbed his head against hers.

'What are you doing?' she said.

'Remember when we used to try to give each other nits so we could get a day off school, by rubbing our heads like this?'

'Get off!' shouted Min, jumping up.

'Want to do a Maori greeting?' Keith said. 'Press foreheads together?'

He pushed his face towards her. She put her hand up in a NO sign.

'Keith, you're obsessed with my head. You are still trying to steal my brain, admit it.'

'No way. No. Wrong. I just want to be friendly. A massage, a chat about the old days, a Maori greeting … '

'Give up, Keith,' said Min. 'Stick to your own life, seriously. It's fine as it is. You're fine as you are.'

It was nice of Min to say that, Keith thought, but it wasn't going to get him to the Inventors' Fair.

Keith kept trying to get close to Min all afternoon, hoping for some brainwave hopping to occur. He took her cups of tea, offered to clean her room, hugged her.

At dinner, he sat very close to her and, after pudding, rested his head on her shoulder.

'Just relaxing with my sister,' he said.

'No, just being weird again,' Min said, shoving him so hard he fell off his chair.

'Or silly,' said his dad.

'Yes, there's been a lot of silliness lately, Keith,' said his mum. 'You're a bad influence on Min.'

'I'm actually trying to be more like her,' Keith said.

'I'm afraid that's unlikely,' said Keith's

mum. 'Min walked at age one, could read age two and by three had written her first collection of poems ... '

'At four she beat adults at chess,' Keith said, 'was an excellent violinist, had set up a weather station in the garden ... Yes, yes, I know, I've heard it all before.'

'*And* she knew her twenty-six times table and was fluent in Italian,' Keith's mum continued. 'I think the most you could do age four is put your trousers on the right way round.'

Back in his room, Keith lay on his bed. Had all Min's genius knowledge passed over, this time?

'What's thirteen multiplied by nine point five?' he asked himself.

Himself had no answer.

He tried to speak Chinese. Nothing came out.

He jumped up and tried some Irish dancing, but stubbed his toe.

He searched his brain for flashes of Min-like genius. There were none.

Instead, his head was dotted with the usual mix of Extremely Important Experiments & Inventions, milkshake dreams and facts about sharks and bears.

Maybe stealing Min's brain would take a little longer. Perhaps it would take a whole night for the brainwaves to cross over. Probably they both needed to be asleep, too, so their sleeping brains could communicate with one another, without distractions.

'If I could just find a way to sleep next to Min, then maybe, by the morning, I'd be a genius too,' Keith said to himself.

That night, once everyone had gone to bed, Keith stood outside Min's room. It was locked, of course, so Keith had to make do with lying down just outside. Close enough? He hoped so. He covered himself with his duvet and fell asleep.

Keith woke to a sharp pain in his ribs, a thudding sound, and a scream. Waking up to screaming seemed to be the norm these days.

'Ow, oww, oww, you idiot!'

It was Min.

'What's happened?' Keith's dad appeared on the landing.

'I was going to the loo and I fell over him. He was lying right there, outside my room!'

'Are you hurt?' Dad said.

'I'm OK,' said Keith, 'though she did kick me quite hard.'

'Not you!' shrieked Dad.

'Min, are you hurt?' said Keith's mum.

'You have a fencing competition next week. Anything broken?'

'What were you even doing on the floor there, Keith?' Dad said. 'Keith? Typical, he's gone.'

Eventually, Keith's parents were satisfied that Min wasn't injured and went back to bed. Moments later, Keith woke to the sound of screaming. Again.

'What are you doing in my bed?' Min screamed. 'How did you even get there?'

Keith was so sleepy he wasn't sure himself. Then he remembered.

'I snuck in while you were being checked over,' he said. 'I just wanted to be near you.'

'Mum! Dad! Keith's being *really* weird again.'

Before his parents could question him, Keith trotted back to his room, pulled the duvet over his head and went back to sleep.

CHAPTER SIX

The next morning, as soon as Keith woke, the terrible truth that he had not managed to steal Min's brain hit him like a big wet flannel in the face. He lay there feeling defeated, then heard Min go to the bathroom for a shower. He tiptoed out on to the landing. Amazingly, she had left her room unlocked. He slipped inside.

The trophies were still gleaming, the

motivational messages still motivating, but this time, Keith noticed all the books. Piles of books. Shelves of books. Books everywhere. Did Min read all of them?

Keith flicked through one of them. It was full of equations. They swam in front of his eyes – dancing numbers and whirling symbols. He opened another. This time the text was tiny, two columns on each page, and the paper as thin as butterfly wings.

Keith spread his hands over the books, stroking them softly. He took a deep breath and began chanting.

'Come, come, come into my brain.'

He imagined the words flying off the page and into his brain so that he suddenly knew loads of things; all those things that Min knew.

'Come, come, come into my brain!'

Keith waited, then tried to multiply seventy-six by thirteen point five. Without success.

'Come, come ... Oh, what's the use?' Keith muttered and, feeling extra defeated with a topping of gloom, he wandered downstairs to the kitchen, where he found his dad, peering into the bread bin.

'I can see why they call it a bread *bin*,' he said. 'This is a load of old bread rubbish.'

This got Keith thinking. He found a pot of furniture varnish in the shed and was painting it on to a slice of white bread when Keith Sr came over, with Peanuts the parrot on his shoulder.

'What are you doing?' Keith Sr asked.

'Waterproofing bread,' said Keith.

'Why?' Keith Sr asked.

'Partly because it's taking my mind off the

fact that I haven't stolen Min's brain, so I still don't have the money to get to the Inventors' Fair. But also, it's because we waste a lot of bread in this house,' said Keith. 'I'm trying to find a use for it. If it was water-proofed, it could be turned into cups and bowls.'

'Nice idea,' said Keith Sr.

'Mum would probably say it was silly. She thinks all my inventions and experiments are silly. Dad does, too.'

'I think they're cool,' said Keith Sr. 'They're genius in their own way. They show you're curious. It's important to be curious.'

'Thanks,' said Keith.

'Your parents maybe don't understand the way you do things. They're focused on Min, and her kind of genius. But that doesn't mean that's the only kind. People *don't* always realise what a genius is. I remember a friend who did an act in the arts clubs. Called himself The Milkman. He would drink a bottle of milk onstage, then another and another. In the end, the milk would spill all over his face and clothes. He couldn't gulp it down fast enough. I thought it was genius, but a lot of people didn't get it.'

'What happened to him?' asked Keith.

'He lost the love for his art – went to work in a bank. Plus, he developed a dairy intolerance, so that didn't help.'

'Stilton!' shrieked Peanuts.

'Why don't you leave that varnish to dry and we'll watch some TV,' said Keith Sr.

Normally Keith and Keith Sr liked to watch *Meet & Tuveg*, about the crime-fighting duo Detective Meet and Inspector Tuveg, but they were up to date with all the latest episodes, so Keith Sr flicked through the channels, eventually landing on a quiz show.

Three serious-looking grown-ups sat behind desks answering serious questions. As the quiz credits rolled, a voice said:

'That's the last in the present series of *Mega Brain* but if you'd like to take part in a special under-fourteens version, *Junior Mega Brain*, please go to our website to apply.'

'That's the kind of competition I need to be on, Grandad!' Keith said. 'I bet you win giant cheques on that.'

'Oh sure,' said Keith Sr, 'and you'd be a star, too. Everyone would know you're a genius then.'

'I don't know enough stuff, though,' said Keith. 'I don't have Min's brain. I failed.'

'Whoa, there, don't use the F word,' said Keith Sr. 'Failed? You only fail if you don't try, and then try some more. Why not apply anyway? Maybe you're more of a genius than you realise. You won't know unless you give it a go.'

CHAPTER SEVEN

Keith Sr's words, about being more of a genius than he realised, bounced around Keith's brain all morning like a ping-pong ball in a washing machine. Later, in the park, he told Tom he was thinking of applying for *Junior Mega Brain* on TV.

'Keith Senior reckons I should try it. Imagine winning that. There would definitely be a giant cheque then.'

'The cheque is giant or the amount of money is giant?' asked Tom.

'Both!' said Keith.

Tom was about to answer when he suddenly noticed loads of pigeons, strutting around them.

'Why are there so many pigeons?' he asked.

'They know I've got Marmite with me,' said Keith.

He pulled out a pot from his pocket.

'Pigeons like Marmite?' Tom said.

'Oh yeah. They like jam, too, but only in the mornings.'

'How do you know this?' Tom asked.

'I did an experiment about what pigeons like to eat,' said Keith. 'It's all logged in my Extremely Important Experiments and Inventions Book.'

'Genius!' said Tom.

'Ha! You said it!'

'It just slipped out!' Tom protested.

'You said it though! You do think I'm a genius. I'm definitely applying for that quiz now.'

Keith whooped, slapped Tom on the back and ran home.

Once upstairs, Keith stood outside Min's bedroom. The sound of wailing came from inside. It made a change from screaming.

'Are you OK?' he asked. 'Did you trap your hair in the door?'

'Go away, I'm listening to Chinese opera,' Min shouted.

'I can't go away, I need to borrow your laptop,' Keith said.

'What for?' Min asked, peering round her door.

'Nothing, just a thing,' said Keith.

'Well, is it nothing, or is it a thing?' Min asked. 'Can't be both, can it?'

'It's a thing,' said Keith. 'Happy? Can I borrow it now?'

Min passed it through the door.

'That music is terrible, by the way,' Keith said, then ducked back into his room.

Keith went to the *Junior Mega Brain* website and began filling out the application form. He was so involved in it, he didn't hear Min coming up behind him.

She flicked his earlobe. He spun round.

'Don't do this,' she said, pointing at the screen.

'Why not?' said Keith.

'No, no, no, brother,' she said. 'The *Junior Mega Brain* quiz is not for people like you. You would be eaten alive.'

'No, I wouldn't,' said Keith. 'I know how to

defend myself against a bear.'

'And me?' Min asked. 'Can you defend yourself against me? I'm already through to the final. I won it last year, so I'm automatic- ally in.'

'You won it last year?' Keith asked. 'I didn't know that.'

'You did, Keith, you came to the after-show party. You didn't speak to anyone, though, because you were too busy lying under a table eating mini egg sandwiches.'

'I'm sure I'd remember eating sandwiches made with Mini Eggs.'

'The *sandwiches* were mini. Anyway, you won't get into the auditions writing that sort of stuff on the application form,' she said. 'Interests: how to weigh hair and eyelashes ... '

'That's important stuff,' said Keith.

'No, it's just stuff you're interested in,' she said. 'To get on to a child-genius quiz, you need to talk about chemistry, geology, ancient civilisations, the Industrial Revolution in England, biodiversity, chess, opera, fencing, the Roman Empire, the poems of Flannery McFlannery O'Clonarty, maths, further maths, even further maths, equations, West African flora and fauna, Antarctic expeditions, rare moths, ballet and ... '

As Min paced the room, listing off more of the genius things she knew about, Keith was quietly typing. Finally, her brain was opening up to him, and he was stealing it, right in front of her.

Eventually, she looked up.

'Sorry, I got carried away,' she said.

'No problem,' said Keith.

'You didn't write all that on the form, did you?' Min asked.

She leaned in and saw that this was exactly what Keith had done.

'Keith …!'

Too late. Keith hit the button marked **SUBMIT APPLICATION** and slammed the laptop shut.

CHAPTER EIGHT

Keith wasn't sure how long it would take to hear about the quiz, but the next day, he decided to prepare anyway. If Keith Sr was right and he was more of a genius than he realised, maybe now was a good time to organise some of his genius thoughts on paper. He grabbed a notebook, then wrote the simple but, he felt, classically genius title of **THE BOOK OF KEITH.**

Inside he wrote some early findings.

Do not expect the world to realise you are a
genius straight away. Remember, everyone else is
not as brilliant as you are. Give them a chance. It
may take them a while to catch on. But - don't
give up. GENIUSES NEVER GIVE UP!

Stealing your sister's brain is not easy. Or your
brother's (if you have one - I don't). Probably,
stealing anyone's brain is not easy. But it's worth
listening in to them, in case they let some genius
nuggets drop.

Then Keith began watching clips of previous *Junior Mega Brain* episodes. There was
Min, firing off answers and getting everything right. Will I be able to do that? Keith
wondered. He struggled to understand the
questions, let alone the answers, and soon

found himself focusing instead on what all the contestants were wearing. There seemed to be a lot of cardigans. Keith wondered what he should wear if he got on to *Junior Mega Brain*. He glanced at his clothes. He was wearing a T-shirt with a tortoise on it, partially covered by a large ketchup stain. The tortoise looked like it was having a nosebleed. He rang Keith Sr about it.

'A strong look is important,' Keith Sr said. 'Make sure people notice you. Make them think, Wow, there's a cool, genius kid right there. Not a suit though. Kids in suits give me the creeps.'

'I get you,' said Keith. 'But what?'

'You can't go wrong with black,' said Keith Sr. 'Maybe some sunglasses, too.'

Keith went upstairs to raid his mum's wardrobe. He found black leggings, a black polo neck and some giant sunglasses with pink frames. He tried them on.

'I look like I'm wearing a wetsuit to the beach,' Keith muttered. 'It's definitely a look. Now I need to try this out – see if people notice me and think, Holy cheesecakes, that kid is a total genius. I'll go and sit in a cafe and drink coffee. Geniuses go mad for coffee, I bet.'

At the cafe in the park, Keith could hardly see Bruce, the owner, even though Bruce was built like an industrial wheelie bin. The sunglasses made everything too dark.

'Coffee, please,' Keith said.

'Certainly, madam,' said Bruce.

Keith found a table outside. He sat down and crossed his legs. He was sure geniuses crossed their legs. Then Bruce brought the coffee. Keith took a sip.

'BLUURGGHH!' Keith spat out a giant arc of coffee, which splattered a man sitting opposite.

'Hey! Do you mind … ?' the man yelled, looking as if he'd spotted a fly in his cornflakes.

Keith did mind.

Coffee tasted disgusting.

Like rust and celery and headache mixed with hot milk. His polo neck was making

him itch and not a single person had looked at him with the respect and admiration a genius deserved. He wandered off, but soon heard footsteps coming up behind him.

He spun round and there was Bruce.

'You left without paying,' he said. 'Hand over the money.'

Keith patted his leggings for change. Nothing.

'Sorry, I don't carry cash,' Keith said. 'Like the Queen.'

'That's not very clever, ordering coffee when you've got no money to pay for it,' said Bruce. 'All right, you can pay me next time.'

Only a stupid person would drink coffee a second time, Keith thought as he trudged home. Then he remembered Bruce had said he was not very clever – the exact opposite of what he wanted to hear. Keith suddenly felt hot and bothered; the polo neck was still itching and his face was burning red. If it had been a paint shade, it would have been called Frustrated Plum. If he did get on the quiz, this would not be the look he'd go for. He would just have to go as himself, normal Keith in jeans and a T-shirt. That would have to do.

Back at home, he made a few more notes in THE BOOK OF KEITH.

Geniuses should not wear polo necks – too itchy.

Geniuses should not drink coffee – very disgusting.

He checked the calendar. The Inventors' Fair was nearly two weeks away now. The *Junior Mega Brain* quiz was his best and only chance of winning the money he needed, but having watched it, and seen all those super-smart kids smashing it, Keith wasn't sure he could even answer his name right, let alone any of the questions. He felt a flicker of hopelessness. Was his dream of going to the fair collapsing like a shed made of marbles? Keith looked at THE BOOK OF KEITH again and one sentence jumped out at him:

GENIUSES NEVER GIVE UP!

Of course! Keith underlined it in red pen, and then went to see what was for dinner.

CHAPTER NINE

The following day, when Keith and Tom returned to Keith's house after a bike ride, they found an envelope on the doormat. Inside was a card, inviting Keith to the auditions of the *Junior Mega Brain* quiz, 'for formidably talented children aged eight to fourteen'.

'I got through!' Keith shouted. 'Holy blob! I got through! Yes!'

Tom was examining the toenail experiment.

His mouth was still twisted into a yuck grimace when he spun round.

'What? Really?' said Tom. 'That's weird, I mean, amazing. Congratulations.'

'This is it!' Keith roared, leaping about on his bed. 'I'm going to win a giant cheque, then I can go to the Inventors' Fair. My dream is about to come true. Oh wow, Mum and Dad will be so impressed, too, when it's me doing the quizzing. Boom!'

He bounced some more then reread the card.

'Hang on a second,' he said. 'The auditions are tomorrow. No time to lose. I need to prepare now.'

'By studying, so you can answer the questions?' Tom asked.

'What? No!' said Keith. 'By baking and working on a new personal fragrance. Here, what do you think of this one?'

Keith passed Tom a bottle. Inside was a liquid that looked a lot like pond water – cloudy and green.

'Smell it,' said Keith.

Tom did and nearly gagged.

'That is *rank*!' he spluttered.

'Actually, it's grassy with a top note of woodsmoke,' said Keith. 'I call it White Nylon.'

'I call it rank,' said Tom.

'White Nylon. It's grassy with a top note of … Oh, never mind,' said Keith. 'I admit it's gone a bit over, so I need to make another one. To really stand a chance in the quiz I need to have a strong personal fragrance. Geniuses take care of how they smell. It's what they do.'

Then Keith grabbed THE BOOK OF KEITH and quickly scrawled in it:

Geniuses always smell excellent.

'Right, let's go to the park,' said Keith. 'I have genius smell work to do. Coming? You might learn something.'

In the park Keith began gathering his 'smell ingredients', which included some grass, some dandelion leaves, a few rose petals and a handful of wood chippings. Back at home, he emptied them on to the kitchen worktop.

'Do you want that bug in your perfume?' Tom asked. 'The one crawling over that rose petal? And that looks like chewing gum, mixed in with the wood chippings.'

Keith wasn't listening. He scooped up all the smell ingredients, poked them into a plastic bottle, and then poured in some water, a squeeze of lemon juice, a teaspoon of washing-up liquid and a drop of blackcurrant squash.

'OK, this needs a few hours to get going.

Perfect. Ready in time for the audition. Now, on to baking.'

'Why baking?' Tom asked.

'It's good to take something when you meet new people, like fresh cakes,' said Keith. 'I'll make Keith's Special Flapjacks.'

'They sound worrying,' said Tom.

'Delicious, more like,' said Keith. 'Pass me the oats.'

Keith got to work. The kitchen quickly became a scene of cooking devastation, with oats scattered everywhere and sugar crunching underfoot. Keith had a butter stain on the front of his T-shirt that was roughly the shape of Africa. Ingredients for Keith's Special Flapjacks, from tea leaves to mashed banana to gravy granules, were strewn across the worktop and the tin of syrup was standing right next to the tin of varnish

Keith had been using to waterproof bread a few days ago.

'Wow, wouldn't want to get those two mixed up!' laughed Tom, pointing at the two tins. But Keith wasn't listening.

'Done,' said Keith, as he popped the flap-jacks in the oven. 'Now I'm ready for the *Junior Mega Brain* audition. Bring it on!'

CHAPTER TEN

Keith Sr had offered to take Keith along to the *Junior Mega Brain* auditions. Keith's dad was at work and his mum was taking Min to a special all-day geology master-class followed by a hula-hooping workshop. They had no idea that their son was trying out for a proper, genius quiz. He hadn't told them.

'How about we fire up *Drifter*,' said Keith Sr.

'The TV studios are right by the canal, after all.'

So, at 7.30 in the morning, Keith strode down the towpath towards Keith Sr's barge and hopped aboard. *Drifter*'s engine rumbled to life and they set off down the canal. Keith Sr was wearing his purple cape. He always wore a purple cape to drive *Drifter*. No one knew why.

'Cheddar cheese!' Peanuts squawked.

Keith stood at the front, his bag on the deck beside him, containing his special flapjacks, his new fragrance – Musk Oxygen: The Smell of a Genius – THE BOOK OF KEITH, and some crisp sandwiches, which Keith Sr had made for him.

'Hunger is the enemy of genius,' he had said. Keith had made a note of this in THE BOOK OF KEITH.

They cruised upriver for some time, then Keith Sr suddenly threw *Drifter* into reverse.

'That bridge is too low,' he said. 'I can't go any further. You jump off now. It's not far to the TV studios. I'll catch you up once I've found somewhere to moor up.'

Keith grabbed his bag and hopped on to the towpath. He ran all the way to the studios and arrived puffed out and hot. His face had gone the Frustrated Plum shade again.

'You're five minutes late,' said one of the *Junior Mega Brain* team. 'Never mind. I'm Ellie. Did you come on your own?'

'My grandad's coming, too,' said Keith. 'He's just parking his barge.'

'I see … I think,' she said. 'Come this way.'

Ellie took Keith to a large room where lots of other young people were waiting. They all looked serious and had serious-looking

grown-ups with them, too. Keith overheard one dad saying to his son, 'Losing is not an option.' Keith noticed that none of these grown-ups were dressed in a purple cape with a parrot on their shoulder.

'Let me explain the pattern of the day,' Ellie said. 'This is the audition stage. Anyone who gets through will go into the first round of the *Junior Mega Brain* quiz, which will be televised. First, we will interview you to camera and find out a bit about you. Most people get through this easily. I mean, unless you say something *really* crazy.'

Keith smiled weakly.

'Then we'll have a mini quiz, sitting on set and using the buzzers,' she continued. 'You'll be playing against two other contestants. If you win, you're through. Any questions?'

Keith sat and watched some of the

children doing their interviews. One boy was asked why he wanted to win the quiz.

'In life, you're always competing against other people. If you don't push yourself, you're not going to win,' he said.

Wow, thought Keith, I'd never thought about life that way before.

Then a girl was asked what winning meant to her.

'Everything,' she said. 'People remember number one. They don't remember number two.'

Is that right? Keith wondered. He tried to think of some equally impressive things to say when it was his turn, but before he could come up with anything, his name was called.

'Hello, Keith, tell me how you spend your spare time,' the interviewer said.

'I do experiments with toenails,' Keith

said. 'And also, about what spreads birds like to eat. I find out cool facts, like a snail can sleep for three years. I watch detective shows, too. *Meet and Tuveg* is my favourite.'

'Why do you want to win *Junior Mega Brain*?'

'The prize money,' said Keith.

The interviewer looked shocked.

'Which I would probably, er, give to charity … ?' he added.

The interviewer smiled.

'Congratulations. You're through to the quiz stage of the audition.'

CHAPTER ELEVEN

Keith watched more children called things like Tarquin and Luna be interviewed about their passion for winning, then went and sat in a corner to eat his salt and vinegar crisp sandwiches.

'Still no sign of Keith Senior. Where is he?' he muttered to himself.

Keith felt a tiny bit lonely. He thought of Min. It would have been great if she were here, to give him some advice and support. Or Mum and Dad, cheering him on. All the other kids had parents with them. Admittedly, they all looked super tense. They kept telling their children to 'focus on victory' and 'not surrender'; to 'keep their foot on the gas' and 'don't slip up now' – that kind of thing. But still ...

'Keith Keithstofferson, please,' one of the assistants called.

It was time for the quiz round. Keith was shown to his seat, behind a long desk with screens in it. He felt a pulse of excitement as his fingers quivered over the buzzer.

A girl sat on his left. She was wearing a cardigan and her hair was scraped back into a neat ponytail. She was biting her nails.

'You look like you know about nails,' Keith said to her. 'You obviously like chewing them.

What do you reckon, can they survive outside the body? I'm doing this experiment and … '

A look of panic spread across the girl's face. She chewed her nails even faster.

'Here, have one of my special flapjacks instead,' Keith said.

He passed her the box. She took one nervously and nibbled a corner like a hamster tackling a particularly large carrot.

'Ooh, it's, um, a rather unusual flavour,' she said. 'I need some water.'

She poured herself a glass from the jug on the desk and gulped it down.

'Oh, help, I can still taste it. An extra-ordinary chemical flavour,' she said, refilling the glass and drinking more.

'That might be the gravy granules,' Keith said, but then remembered the varnish tin and the golden syrup tin side by side on the kitchen worktop, and felt a flicker of doubt.

'I'm Keith, by the way.'

The girl ignored him and drank a third glass of water, gargling it before swallowing.

'Diabolical,' she muttered.

'Pleased to meet you,' said Keith. 'All right if I call you Di?'

Keith then turned to the other contestant.

'Flapjack?'

'No thanks, I don't eat sugar,' said the boy. 'It inhibits my mental function.'

'Crelion, do not touch those cakes!' shouted a woman in the audience.

'It's fine, Mummy, I haven't had one,' he called back.

'Cakes and cookies are absolutely one hundred per cent forbidden, remember. Even on your birthday. *Especially* on your birthday! And why is that?'

'The only sweetness we crave is the sweet taste of success,' Crelion said.

'Louder!' said his mum.

'The only sweetness we crave is the sweet taste of success!' Crelion repeated, louder, but also blushed a bit.

Keith started laughing. Crelion glared at him.

'I'll save you one in case you change your mind,' Keith whispered. 'Did you know foxes like sandwiches?'

Before Crelion could answer, there was a cry from the audience:

'Brie, Brie!'

'Peanuts!' Keith yelled. 'And Keith Senior, you made it.'

He waved at them as they sat down, and then the lights dimmed. Another of the young assistants sat down in the quizzing chair. She was carrying a thick wad of cards with questions printed on them.

'Welcome to the auditions of *Junior Mega Brain*,' she said. 'We will start with the solo rounds. Each contestant has to answer as many questions as possible in just forty-five seconds. I wish you all luck. We will begin with Crelion. So, if you're ready, your forty-five seconds starts now.'

CHAPTER TWELVE

Crelion knew a lot. Really a lot. With every correct answer, his mum punched the air, then waited anxiously for the next question, her hands clasped in front of her in a tense knot.

Keith felt a flutter in his stomach. Nerves? Surely geniuses didn't get nervous? Maybe he was hungry. He glanced at the flapjacks. The girl next to him was still swigging water after eating some. She had drunk about six glasses.

'Saffy, now it's your turn,' said the quizmaster.

BUZZZ!

It was Keith.

'She's called Di, not Saffy,' he said. 'Full name: Diablitical, or something. Just so you know. Wow, these buzzers are seriously loud.'

Some of the parents in the audience tutted loudly.

Peanuts squawked 'Brie!' again.

'No more interruptions, please,' said the quizmaster. 'Saffy, your forty-five seconds starts now.'

Saffy also knew a lot, just like Crelion. Keith's stomach flipped again. He reached for the flapjacks, but there was no time. The spotlight was on him now.

'Are you ready?' the quizmaster asked.

'No, I'm Keith,' he said, and laughed. Nobody else did.

'Actually, no I'm not, ready that is,' he said. 'I forgot to put on my new perfume – Musk Oxygen: The Smell of a Genius.'

Keith rummaged in his bag and found the bottle. The perfume had gone a worrying shade of brown. Without pausing to sniff it, Keith sloshed some into his palm and smeared it on his face.

'Oh, my word, what is that terrible stink?' said Crelion.

'Musk Oxygen, my new fragrance,' said Keith. 'It's important to smell the part, don't you think? I think it smells amazing. Plus, this is nowhere near as powerful as my previous fragrances, White Nylon and Serious Lycra.'

'Your forty-five seconds starts now,' said the quizmaster. 'What's another name for a narrow path or route between mountains?'

Keith shook his head.

'Pass,' he said.

'Correct.'

'Sweet!' said Keith.

'The poet Berty Bosh Swelly famously had a blind pet deer. What was its name?'

'No idea,' said Keith.

'Correct.'

'Achooo,' went Crelion. 'That stinking perfume is making me sneeze.'

'What Italian cheese is famous for its blue veining and strong flavour?'

'Gorgonzola!' screeched Peanuts. Keith didn't even have to open his mouth.

'Correct,' said the quizmaster.

Saffy took another glug of water, still

hoping to wash the terrible flapjack taste away. Crelion sneezed loudly and rubbed his eyes.

'Complete the following famous quote from the play *Hamlet*: "To be or not to be ... "'

'What is the question?' Keith asked.

'It's "*that* is the question", but I'll give you the point,' said the quizmaster.

BEEP BEEP BEEP.

The forty-five seconds were over.

'That brings us to the end of your solo round, Keith. You have four points,' she said. 'Crelion and Saffy also have four points each.'

The audience clapped.

'Now, on to the quick-fire round, where anyone can answer,' said the quizmaster. 'Fingers on buzzers, please. Name the country highlighted in red on your screen.'

'I can't see it,' Crelion protested, wiping

his eyes and sneezing again.

Saffy was fidgeting in her chair and not looking at the screen.

'It's Azerbaijan,' said the quizmaster. 'Next question. Franz Flupple's famous painting of Queen Mary shows her holding what?'

'Atishoo!' Crelion sneezed.

'No, not a tissue, it was a sword,' said the quizmaster.

Crelion blinked rapidly. His eyelids were puffy and red now.

'What were the famous last words of Admiral Lord Knockerbox?' continued the quizmaster.

BUZZZ!

'I'm going to wet myself,' said Saffy.

'Incorrect.'

'No, I really am going to wet myself,' said Saffy. She jumped up from her seat and ran offstage. The audience gasped.

'When you've got to go, you've got to go,' said Keith.

'For what role is TV actor Malcolm Major best known?'

Finally, a question Keith was sure of.

BUZZ!

'Inspector Tuveg!' he shrieked. 'From *Meet and Tuveg*!'

'Correct,' said the quizmaster.

'That's my grandson,' Keith Sr said proudly to the woman sitting next to him.

BEEP BEEP BEEP.

'And that's the end of the quick-fire round. Looking at the scores, I can see that Keith, you have the most points. Congratulations, you're through to the first round of *Junior Mega Brain*.'

Keith leaped up from his chair and punched the air, shouting, 'YES! YES! YES!'

Keith Sr whooped and cheered from the audience and Peanuts flew around the studio, doing tiny parrot droppings all over it.

'Not fair,' shouted Crelion. 'His stupid perfume made me sneeze and made my eyes water. I couldn't see.'

'And I had to drink so much water to get the horrid taste of his special flapjacks out of my mouth that I needed the toilet and missed the last question,' said Saffy.

'I'm afraid it's the contestants' responsibility to get to the toilet in time and to take care of any allergies they may have before coming on to the quiz,' said the quizmaster. 'Keith is through, and that's that.'

CHAPTER THIRTEEN

Once home, Keith tapped on his sister's door. She unlocked it and poked her head round.

'What?' she said. Then she caught a whiff of Keith.

'You stink! Have you been making horrible perfumes again?'

'That's no way to talk to a contestant in the first round of *Junior Mega Brain*,' Keith said.

Min's mouth fell open.

'You're joking,' she said. 'You went to the auditions? And got through? What? How?'

'I just cruised through, easy as beans.'

'You mean you cheated?' said Min. 'Or the other contestants were really dumb, or ill or something?'

'They were super smart and knew loads,

but in the end, I was just the bigger genius,' said Keith. 'Want a flapjack?'

Min bit into one and immediately spat it out.

'That's vile!' she said.

'Hmm, that's what one of the contestants said. She mentioned a chemical flavour. Might be varnish, I'm not sure … '

'Wait, you gave flapjacks made with varnish to one of the contestants?' Min asked. 'No wonder she couldn't answer the questions with this taste in her mouth. Did anyone else eat them?'

'No, but the guy sitting next to me was rude about my new perfume. Said it stinks. He kept sneezing.'

'So, you poisoned one and made the other have an allergic reaction,' said Min. '*That's* how you got through the audition. And let's not forget, you only got to the audition in the first place by filling out the form with all my interests. You basically stole my brain.'

'But I won,' Keith protested.

'Well, you're going to need more than dodgy cakes and a bad smell to get through to the final,' said Min. 'Now get out of my room, you're far too pongy.'

'It's Musk Oxygen: The Smell of a Genius,' Keith said, but Min had already shut the door in his face.

Did Min have a point? Had Keith only got through because of his flapjacks and perfume? He felt doubt nibbling at him like a terrible squirrel, the kind of terrible squirrel that makes you really doubt yourself. He was still thinking about it the next day, when he went into the kitchen to make some toast. One of Min's maths books was on the table. He approached it slowly and, using just one finger, like he was half expecting something nasty to jump out, opened it.

'Every square number is the sum of two or more consecutive odd numbers,' Keith read.

He slammed the book shut.

'No thank you.'

Then he remembered what he'd written in THE BOOK OF KEITH – Geniuses never give up.

Keith opened the book again, took a deep breath, and began reading about tangents and trigonometry. He read for a minute, maybe two, before feeling a tremendous urge to smack himself in the face with some oven gloves.

Once he'd done this, Keith decided to go to the library. Maybe the books there would be more useful and inspiring. He spent a happy hour wandering around the many shelves, picking up books at random. Which is why he left with *Moss Growing for Beginners* and *A Brief History of Crisps*.

Back in his room, Keith sat at his desk and began jotting down what he felt were important facts or, as he liked to call them, Keith's Nuggets.

When Min came in later, she read one.

'Barbecued kangaroo is a flavour of crisp.'

'That's one of Keith's Nuggets,' said Keith, beaming.

'It's a nice nugget, but it won't come up in the quiz,' she said.

Keith sighed.

'There's a maths round, a words round and a general knowledge round,' said Min. 'That's what you need to be reading about.'

'Sounds like a lot,' Keith said.

'It is,' said Min. 'I have hundreds of books in my room on all those subjects.'

'Have you read them all?' Keith asked.

'Yes, of course,' said Min. 'I've been studying all my life.'

'When do you watch *Meet and Tuveg*?'

'I don't know what that is,' said Min.

'What about seeing friends?'

'I don't have many,' said Min. 'The kids I meet at competitions are so competitive it's hard to get on with them. It's all "I have to win, I must win, get out of my way I'm off to do some more winning".'

Keith nodded.

'This is *not* how I thought being a genius was at all,' he said. 'I thought being a genius was easy. Sounds like it's actually very full on. I didn't realise how full on your life is. It's extremely full on.'

'Stop saying full on,' said Min.

Keith patted Min's head.

'Are you trying to steal my brain again?' Min asked.

'No, just showing some respect for it. That's a hard-working brain up there,' he said.

Min read out another of Keith's Nuggets.

'Mosses are springy and feel nice to walk on. That's more an opinion than a fact. It won't come up.'

'Well, what will come up then?' Keith asked.

'How do I know?' said Min. 'I'm clever, but I can't see into the future.'

'Not that clever then … ' Keith muttered. 'Look, sis, the first round of the quiz is the day after tomorrow. I really need to win, get to the final, then win again and get the prize money. It's my last chance to go to the Inventors' Fair. What should I do? Can I borrow some books?

Maybe if all I do is read books between now and then I'll be fine.'

'Cramming, you mean?' said Min. 'That doesn't work. It's no replacement for putting in the hours.'

'I don't have "the hours",' said Keith. 'I am totally running out of "the hours". I have hardly any of "the hours" left at all. You have to help me!'

'All right, all right, calm down,' said Min. 'You can borrow some books, but I'm not sure that will help.'

'Well, it's all I've got,' said Keith. 'It's worth a go, isn't it?'

CHAPTER FOURTEEN

The next morning, Keith woke up under a pile of books. He was still in his clothes. He squinted around the room. There were books everywhere. It looked like a hurricane in a library.

Sleepily, he began to piece things together:
- how he had started reading the books Min had given him;
- how he had struggled to understand one,

thrown it aside and begun on another;

- how he had lost track of time as he wrestled with complex facts;
- how it had felt like a huge gorilla was dragging him through syrup into a black hole;
- how he had eventually fallen asleep.

Keith heard squawking and cries of 'Mozzarella' and Peanuts fluttered into the room, followed by Keith Sr.

'I brought you a bun,' said Keith Sr.

'A bun? There's no time for buns. I've got to study,' Keith said.

Then Min appeared.

'How's it going?' she asked.

'How do you think it's going? Terribly!' he said. 'There's too much to learn. Too many dates and numbers and facts.'

'I did warn you that cramming doesn't work,' Min said.

Keith made a sound that was a cross between a growl and a whimper. He kicked some of the books off his bed, then rolled on to his front, burying his face in the pillow.

'What's going on, son?' asked Keith Sr, gently rolling him back over again.

'I was studying all night, trying to learn genius stuff,' said Keith. 'But it's impossible. I thought I could be a genius and win money for the Inventors' Fair. But it's all gone wrong. I can't do it. I can't. I'm just not like Min.'

'No, you're like you, which is great. You know a lot of stuff already, remember? And you're creative. Who else would think to waterproof bread?'

'That's true,' Keith sniffed. 'And I discovered that pigeons eat Marmite and foxes like sandwiches.'

'So, there you go. That's a lot of thinking

going on,' said Keith Sr, gently tapping Keith's head. 'Now you get some sleep, and tomorrow, all you have to do is give it your best shot. Remember, I'll be in the audience cheering you on. Peanuts, too. Just be you. You might surprise yourself.'

After his grandad had tucked him in, Keith fell into a deep sleep and awoke, several hours later. Following Keith Sr's advice, he took the rest of the day off. He ate his bun, went for a nice stroll in the park, called in on Tom and added a bit more wisdom to THE BOOK OF KEITH (Geniuses eat buns). He did not do any more studying.

In the evening, Keith Sr rang him up.

'How are you doing?' he asked.

'Not bad,' said Keith. 'I rested today, like you said, so I feel pretty good. I really, really want to win the quiz tomorrow. You know what that prize money would mean to me, but all I can do is try, in my own way.'

'That's right, son,' said Keith Sr. 'All you can do is Keep It Keith.'

Keith laid out his outfit for the next day before he went to bed. He had found a pair of very old pants at the back of his drawer that were so faded that they could just about pass for yellow. He knew Min had been joking about wearing yellow pants for luck, but she still had her lucky socks, didn't she? Even though they were too small and very tight, Keith now had lucky pants.

Then he laid out a T-shirt and jeans – no sunglasses, no polo neck. Just Keith, being Keith, dressed as Keith. It would have to do.

CHAPTER FIFTEEN

The next morning, Keith Sr met Keith at the bus stop – no barges and low bridges today, although Keith Sr was still wearing his purple cape, with Peanuts perched on his shoulder – and they travelled to the TV studios.

They were shown backstage, where the tension lay thickly in the air, like royal icing on an expensive Christmas cake.

'You must focus,' one dad was whispering to his nervous son. 'Don't think of anything except winning. Nothing else exists.'

A girl was chewing her long hair and a boy in the corner was pacing up and down while his mum said he 'couldn't afford to mess up now'.

Suddenly the room went quiet. A tall boy with dark eyes and wavy black hair strode in. While most of the children were wearing some kind of cardigan, this boy wore a leather jacket and white T-shirt. The other contestants gazed at him admiringly. So did their parents.

'Who's that?' Keith asked the hair-chewing girl.

'That's Patterson Patterson,' she whispered.

'Funny name,' Keith said.

'He's a genius,' said the girl.

Well, durr, Keith thought to himself, but didn't say anything.

Patterson Patterson sat in a corner, crossed his legs and stared straight in front of him, completely calm, completely alone. There was no anxious mum or dad with him, telling him he had to keep his foot on the gas. And no grandad with a parrot either.

'Iceman,' Keith muttered.

A door swung open at the far end of the room. Keith went and peered through, and found he was looking straight into the studio itself. There were huge cameras, lots of lights, studio staff running around adjusting things, and then there was the audience, and it was massive. Hundreds of people, all waiting.

A producer gathered the children together and explained that they would be called up one at a time to do the maths round first, then words, then general knowledge. She pointed out where they would sit, to the side of the stage, in full view of the cameras.

'That means no picking your nose,' Keith joked, nudging the hair-chewing girl. She yelped like she'd had her ice cream stolen by a seagull, then carried on chewing her hair.

The children were given name badges. There was a Titus, two Persephones (one hair chewing), a Lark and Patterson Patterson, but no other Keiths. Keith was the only Keith.

'Good luck, son,' said Keith Sr. 'Keep It Keith.'

The child geniuses were shown to their seats.

The presenter, Robert Bobbinson, walked on to the set. He was tall, bald and looked extremely stern, like a librarian who's caught someone eating chips in the non-fiction section.

'He seems a bit scary,' Keith whispered to Titus.

Titus gulped nervously.

The quiz started. Titus, the two Persephones and Lark answered their maths questions. Keith felt this went on forever. Just when he thought he would prefer to stick a poisonous jellyfish down his too-small-and-not-quite-yellow lucky pants than hear any more, Patterson Patterson strolled up to the podium. He was much taller than all the other contestants. The audience seemed to sit up and take notice. He looked out at them, as cool and calm as a cool, calm cucumber, but Keith thought his eyes were like a shark's – lifeless.

Patterson Patterson sailed through his maths round with no mistakes, like a robot.

'Nice one, congratulations,' Keith whispered to him when he retook his seat.

Patterson Patterson raised his hand in a stop sign. 'Don't break my concentration,' he said. 'Nobody breaks my concentration.'

Then Robert Bobbinson spoke again.

'And now I'd like to welcome to the podium Keith Keithstofferson.'

Finally, it was Keith's turn.

CHAPTER SIXTEEN

'Your sixty seconds starts now,' said Robert Bobbinson. 'What is four squared, times two, plus sixteen?'

'Good question,' said Keith. 'It's probably quite a lot, isn't it?'

'Please answer the question,' said Robert Bobbinson.

'Over four hundred but under six hundred?' said Keith.

'Please answer the question,' said Robert Bobbinson again.

'Can you give me a clue?' Keith said.

Someone in the audience laughed. Robert Bobbinson glowered.

'I've forgotten the numbers,' said Keith. 'Four times something, wasn't it? I'll come back to that.'

More laughing in the audience.

'What is seventy-five divided by the square root of twenty-five?' said Robert Bobbinson.

'Ooh, tricky,' said Keith. 'I'd need to use a calculator for that one.'

'Calculators are not permitted in this round,' Robert Bobbinson barked. 'Next question. What's twelve times three, plus half that number, plus thirteen?'

Keith blinked.

'I don't think I'm going to be able to answer

that, Bobbin,' said Keith. 'Sorry.'

There were giggles from the audience.

'What is he doing?' one Persephone whispered to the other.

'We can just wrap it up now if you like,' said Keith. 'Or you could answer a question of mine. What's with the serious face, Bobby?'

More gasps.

'It's Robert. Not Bobbin or Bobby.'

'Sorry, Robin. I just mean, most of these other contestants are pretty stressed as it is, apart from old Pat-a-cake Pat-a-cake. But the problem is, you're making it worse.'

Robert Bobbinson stared hard at Keith but said nothing.

'It's so tense. We need to lighten the mood,' said Keith.

Someone in the audience shouted 'Yeah'.

BEEP BEEP BEEP.

'Keith, you've scored a total of no points. Which brings us to the end of the first round.'

Then Robert Bobbinson marched off.

Keith nodded and muttered 'Fair enough,' but it was drowned out by the sound of clapping. He turned to the audience. He bowed, which made his too-small-and-not-quite-yellow lucky pants pinch unpleasantly, but he didn't mind, because the audience clapped even harder.

In fact, they were still clapping and smiling when the lights went up and the contestants were ushered out of the studio.

Back in the waiting room, there were sandwiches on a big table, and fruit and jugs of squash, but no one was eating. Patterson Patterson stood in the corner, staring out at the room with his shark eyes, while all the parents were busy coaching their kids. One of the Persephones was sobbing quietly, because she had got one question wrong. Her mum stood next to her, tapping her watch.

'No time for tears, P,' she said. 'While you *cry*, your chances of winning *die*. Remember?'

Some of the contestants looked up shyly as Keith 'No Points' Keithstofferson walked through the room; Titus even chanced a small wave.

Keith found Keith Sr, who wrapped him in

his big purple cape and gave him a hug. Peanuts nibbled his ear and squawked 'Dairylea triangles'.

'I didn't exactly smash that,' said Keith. 'Those questions were *hard*!'

'That's all right, son,' said Keith Sr. 'You were very Keith. It was good to see. And you heard all that clapping, right? The audience loved you.'

A young boy came up to Keith and asked for his autograph.

'You were so cool,' he said. 'The way you just totally didn't know anything? It was awesome.'

'Err . . . Thanks.'

'Are you going to get no points in the next round, too?' said the boy.

Keith bit into his sandwich, but said nothing.

CHAPTER SEVENTEEN

The next round was about words. All the contestants answered as many questions as they could, but none could match Patterson Patterson, who eased into the lead with barely a blink.

'Holy crackers, he's good,' Keith whispered to one of the Persephones.

Finally, Keith was called up to the podium.

'Hello again,' he said. 'Hope everyone had

a nice lunch. Did you try those cheese sand-wiches? They were delicious. Some kind of excellent pickle in them.'

There was laughter from the audience. Titus and Lark seemed more excited, too. There was a fizz of anticipation in the air. Everyone was looking at Keith. Except Patterson Patterson, who stared straight ahead.

'Shall we begin?' said Robert Bobbinson.

'Yes, we shall,' said Keith.

A woman in the audience sniggered.

'It's OK, you can laugh,' said Keith. 'It was super tense around here this morning. Everyone needs to relax a bit.'

One of the Persephones giggled nervously.

'You have sixty seconds starting now. What eleven-letter word starting with M describes a person who likes to play tricks on others?'

'Someone who messes about?' said Keith. 'A messerabouter!'

The audience laughed.

'The answer is: mischievous,' said Robert Bobbinson. 'What seven-letter word starting with D means to interrupt someone when they are doing something?'

'Debother? Debungle? Debutt-in-on?'

The audience laughed again.

'Disturb,' said Robert Bobbinson.

'What nine-letter word beginning with W means something or someone extremely good?'

'Well good?' said Keith. 'Weally nice? Wicked? No, that's not nine letters. Umm . . . hang on, I know this … '

'Wonderful,' said Robert Bobbinson.

'It will be once I remember the answer,' said Keith.

The people in the audience laughed really hard now.

'No, wonderful *is* the answer,' said Robert Bobbinson. 'What six-letter word beginning with T describes someone who treats people in a cruel and unfair way?'

'Turnip?' said Keith.

'Tyrant,' said Robert Bobbinson.

'Too bad,' said Keith.

More laughter.

BEEP BEEP BEEP.

'At the end of that round, Keith, you have a total of no points,' said Robert Bobbinson.

The audience clapped frantically and whooped. The sound filled the studio. Someone shouted, 'Go, Keith.' Keith bowed again, which made them clap even more (and caused the same pinching issues with his pants).

General knowledge was the final round of

the quiz. The Persephones, Lark and Titus all seemed less uptight now. They smiled. They waved at the audience. Keith had brought some sunshine into the serious world of child-genius quizzing.

Then Patterson Patterson took to the podium. The audience hushed a little. He answered his questions without a flicker of hesitation. He was like a sports car overtaking a line of lorries on the motorway. The audience clapped politely.

Next, a ripple of excitement travelled through the audience when everyone realised Keith was next. As Keith got up, one person began chanting 'Keith, Keith', then another, until it seemed everybody was shouting his name. When Keith finally reached the podium, the audience erupted into applause.

'Quiet,' said Robert Bobbinson.

'Come on, Keith!' shouted one of the audience.

'You can do it, Keith!' shouted another.

'Keep It Keith,' Keith Sr shouted.

'Double Gloucester!' squawked Peanuts.

Patterson Patterson's shark eyes narrowed into angry slits.

'Silence!' Robert Bobbinson shouted. 'Keith, your sixty seconds starts now. What's the capital city of Cuba?'

'Haven't a clue,' said Keith.

'No, it's Havana,' said Robert Bobbinson.

'That's what I said. *Havana* a clue,' said Keith.

'Give him the point!' someone shouted.

'Yeah, point to Keith, point to Keith!' more people shouted.

Robert Bobbinson paused for a second, then pressed a button on his desk. Keith's score

pinged up to one. There was a huge cheer.

'What is a marmot?'

'Easy! It's a spread for your toast,' said Keith. 'Pigeons love it, by the way.'

'Incorrect. It's a type of large squirrel,' said Robert Bobbinson.

The audience did a loud 'Oohhh' as if they were disappointed.

'What creature appears on the flag of Wales?'

'A whale, maybe?' said Keith. More laughter from the audience. 'I'm not sure, Robert, to be honest, but I know how to defend myself against a bear. Why don't you ask me that?'

'Yeah, ask him that,' someone shouted. 'Go on.'

'I will not ask him how to defend himself against a bear,' said Robert Bobbinson, looking flustered now.

'It's a useful thing to know, Rob,' said Keith. 'Next time you meet a bear you're going to wish you'd asked.'

BEEP BEEP BEEP.

It was the end of the round.

'Keith Keithstofferson, you have a total of one point,' said Robert Bobbinson.

The audience erupted. Chants of 'Keith! Keith!' filled the studio.

Keith waved and smiled, the audience got to its feet, clapping even harder now, and Peanuts flew around squawking 'Wensleydale!'

'I've never seen anything like this before in all my years of quiz hosting,' said Robert Bobbinson.

Patterson Patterson stormed off.

CHAPTER EIGHTEEN

Back at home, Keith sat on his bed and let out a sigh. What a day! The crowd had loved him, and not because he knew lots of facts like Min, but just because he was Keith, being Keith. This was more encouragement in one day than he'd had in ages from his parents. It felt brilliant.

What wasn't brilliant, though, was the fact that Keith hadn't got through to the final.

That meant no prize money and no Inventors' Fair. But at least he had had a go. Keith felt good about himself for that. Maybe he could wash cars after all, and start saving for next year's Inventors' Fair?

Min came into his room.

'You only got one point?' she said. 'That's a disaster.'

'I'd say it was kind of a miracle,' said Keith. 'Everyone was excited for me, though. They knew I wasn't going to win but they still cheered for me.'

'But what will Mum and Dad say when they see you on TV?' said Min. 'If I went on a quiz and got a single, solitary point they'd never ever let me forget it. I'd have to do extra study, extra lessons. I'm shuddering just thinking about it.'

'Well, the quiz is on tomorrow,' said Keith.

'Maybe they'll be impressed that their son can compete with geniuses too?'

They weren't.

When the *Junior Mega Brain* logo flashed across the TV the next day, Keith's mum sat forward in her chair.

'Was that Keith Senior in the audience?' she gasped.

'Wait, that's you, Keith, you're on the show!' his dad said.

'Just sit back and enjoy the ride,' said Keith.

But nobody sat back, and nobody enjoyed the ride. Min was hunched over, with a cushion pressed to her face. Only her eyes and two raised eyebrows could be seen. Keith's mum and dad watched with open mouths and the occasional 'Oh my goodness'.

As the credits rolled, Keith's dad stood up.

'I am speechless,' he said. But he wasn't.

He fired questions at Keith more quickly than Robert Bobbinson had: how on earth did he get on the show, what was he thinking, why had he done this?

'I thought you'd be proud!' said Keith.

'For embarrassing yourself on TV?' said Keith's dad.

'And for embarrassing Min,' said Keith's mum. 'Everyone in the child-genius community will know you're her brother. You did this in front of Patterson Patterson, too, one of the most outstanding child geniuses ever. What must he think of you?'

'Who cares?' said Keith. 'He's boring. The audience liked me, though.'

'They were cheering on a circus clown!' said Keith's dad.

'Did Keith Senior put you up to this?' Mum asked.

'No, it was my idea,' said Keith. 'I applied and got through the audition. I did it all – in my own way.'

'Why, Keith?' Mum said. 'This is Min's world, not yours.'

'I wanted the prize money, to go to the Inventors' Fair in Paris,' said Keith. 'I've wanted to go there since I was six years old. You won't take me. You won't even talk about taking me. It's just no, no, no. Then I realised that Min wins money for her genius stuff and I thought, I could do that too.'

'You were never going to win, though, were you?' said Keith's mum. 'It takes years of study and natural brilliance to win.'

'Well, at least I tried, didn't I?' said Keith.

His parents said nothing. Keith ran upstairs to his room.

CHAPTER NINETEEN

'Whhaaaaa!'

Yet again, Keith woke to the sound of screaming.

This time it was his mum.

'Keith! There are people in the front garden!' she screeched.

Keith opened his eyes. It was 7 a.m. He looked outside. There was a crowd of people standing there.

'What do they want?' Keith mumbled.

'You, I think,' said Min, appearing by his side. 'Your appearance on the quiz caused quite a stir. You're trending on the internet. There are loads of hashtags: #KeithforPM and #KeepItKeith. There's an online petition – people want you in the final.'

Downstairs, Keith's dad was peering out.

'You need to tell these people to leave,' he said. 'They're trespassing. If they're not gone

by the time we get back from Min's Latin and kick-boxing competition, then, well – I don't know what.'

Keith was still half asleep when he opened the front door. His fans rushed forward.

'We thought you were amazing on *Junior Mega Brain* last night,' said one girl. 'Me and my family drove all the way from Scotland in our camper van to see you. We brought our eight rabbits, too.'

Keith noticed some large black-and-white rabbits lolloping across the grass. One sneezed loudly.

'They're Chilean sneezing rabbits,' she said.

A woman with curly grey hair and a cap that said #KeepItKeith pushed through the crowd and hugged him.

'Say some Keith things!' she said.

'Yes, yes,' shouted everyone. 'Say Keith things!'

'I haven't had breakfast yet,' said Keith.

'Amazing!' cried the woman. 'That's so Keith. Say something else.'

'If you want Keith things, you might like my book, **THE BOOK OF KEITH**. It's my thoughts on how to be a genius, but it's not finished yet.'

'That's OK, we can wait,' said the fans.

And they did wait, right there, in the front garden. One man was entertaining everyone by drinking a carton of milk, which splashed down his front, and the Scottish family's rabbits continued nibbling the lawn and sneezing.

When Min and Keith's parents left for Min's Latin and kick-boxing competition, the fans crowded around them, calling them 'Family of Keith'. Keith's dad tripped over a rabbit and landed on a full carton of milk, which exploded over his trousers. He was not happy.

Later that morning, Keith went back outside and asked his fans to leave, but they still said no. Keith said they would get him in trouble, but one fan, an enormous ex-wrestler called Big Puffy, said he'd protect him. Keith then made a poster saying **PLEASE GO HOME** and stuck it in the window, but they just ignored it.

Keith tried to work on **THE BOOK OF KEITH**. If he could finish it and give it to his fans, they might leave, but the genius insights wouldn't come. He decided to go to Keith Sr's barge and work on it there, but as soon as he left the house the fans rushed up to him, asking for 'wisdom'.

Keith had to swiftly retreat inside and call Keith Sr instead.

'I'm trapped. In my own house. There are loads of fans outside. Every time I go out, they scream and crowd around me.'

'Fans? Because of your appearance on the quiz last night? What do they want?' asked Keith Sr.

'To hear my wisdom. To touch my clothes,' said Keith. 'They're totally in the way, and

I'm too scared to go out. Plus, Dad has said they have to be gone by the time he gets home at seven p.m.'

'You just hang tight, little buddy,' said Keith Sr. 'I'm coming over. I'll bring crisp sandwiches, too.'

About half an hour later, Keith watched through the window as Keith Sr picked his way across the front lawn. Everyone crowded around him and called him 'Grandfather of Keith'. They tried to pet Peanuts, too, calling her 'Bird of Grandfather of Keith'. She squawked 'Parmesan' at them and fluttered out of the way. Then Keith Sr paused to hug the man who had been drinking milk, like they were old friends.

'Wow, that was quite something,' said Keith Sr once he was safely inside. 'They really like you. Even my old buddy The

Milkman is out there. Good to see him again. Fans though, eh? Incredible. You're a big deal.'

'But being a genius isn't supposed to be like this. Min's never had crowds of fans on the front lawn.'

'That's what happens when you're just you being you,' said Keith Sr. 'People can see you're pretty special.'

BRING, BRING, BRING.

Keith picked up the phone.

'Keithstofferson residence. Yes. That's me. Oh yes. How much? Are you sure? Say that again. Really? Five, zero, zero? OK. That's amazing. Triple amazing. Extra amazing. Thanks. Thanks so much. Bye.'

Keith hung up.

'You OK?' Keith Sr asked. 'You look dazed.'

'That was the TV company,' Keith said.

'I'm so popular, people are demanding to see me in the final. The TV people are even going to pay me to appear – *five hundred pounds*! Just what I need to go to the Inventors' Fair. I've done it. Prize money! Woohoo!'

CHAPTER TWENTY

Keith was so excited about actually winning a giant cheque that he jumped about on the sofa for three solid minutes.

He wasn't the only one who was excited.

As soon as the news broke that Keith would be on the *Junior Mega Brain* final, Keith's fans started celebrating. They played loud music, the rabbits sneezed even more, and The Milkman kept on tipping milk into his face – oat milk though, on account of his dairy intolerance. Keith went outside and joined them. He spent most of the day dancing with his fans, until Keith Sr told him it was getting late.

'It's nearly seven p.m., son,' he said. 'Your folks and Min will be home soon.'

'Keith Senior's right,' Keith told everyone. 'You all need to leave. Thanks for the support and everything, but can you go now?'

'But we are your loyal fans,' they told him.

'Could you go and be loyal somewhere else?' Keith asked.

The answer was no, despite some full-on pleading from Keith. Eventually, he gave up and went to hide in his room until he heard yet another scream, this time from his dad.

'KEEIITTHHHH! Why are all those people still on my lawn?' he bellowed.

Keith tiptoed downstairs nervously.

'They won't go,' he said. 'I tried. I asked nicely. I made a sign.'

Then Min appeared, holding one of the rabbits.

'Hey, they say you're through to the final of *Junior Mega Brain*,' she said. 'By popular demand.'

'What?' said Keith's dad.

'Loads of people rang into the TV company, begging to see more of Keith, so they have put him through to the final, on a wild card,' Min explained.

'They're going to pay me five hundred pounds,' said Keith. 'It means I can go to the Inventors' Fair.'

Keith's mum looked stunned. Keith's dad looked cross. There was an awkward pause, before Keith's dad exploded:

'Do not even think about appearing in the final of *Junior Mega Brain*, Keith.'

'But Dad! I have to!' Keith protested.

'I will not stand for any more of your silliness. Min is going on and she is going to win.'

'Well, hopefully … ' muttered Min.

'No, you're going to win. *To win is the thing* – remember? But Keith's not going to appear, and those people outside are going to leave my garden, because I'm going to call the police, and that rabbit's going to get out of my house, too, and then we're all going to sit down and have dinner and behave like normal, civilised human beings. Got it?'

Keith's mum and dad marched into the kitchen, leaving Keith, Min and a sneezing rabbit in the hall.

'Wow, Dad's going to do a lot of things,' Min whispered.

'He's going to get cross, then he's going to have a tantrum, then he's going to chuck a rabbit out, then he's going to ring the fire brigade … ' whispered Keith.

'Seriously, though, what will you do about the quiz?' Min asked. 'Dad says you can't do it.'

'Are you kidding? That's my ticket to the Inventors' Fair – literally,' Keith said. 'Plus, appearing on the quiz again will be awesome fun.'

Min put the rabbit back outside, and the two of them stood on the doorstep as Keith's fans chanted 'Keep It Keith! Keep It Keith!'

Keith laughed and grinned. He tried to shush them, but the fans kept on chanting his name. Keith waved and blew kisses, and when he finally looked around, Min had gone.

CHAPTER
TWENTY-ONE

Keith found Min in her room.

'What's up?' he asked.

'You don't take anything seriously, do you?' she said. 'Everything's just a laugh to you, including the *Junior Mega Brain* quiz.'

'And everything's so serious to you and Dad and Mum,' said Keith. 'What's wrong with having fun?'

Min didn't answer.

'Holy crumpets,' Keith said. 'You're jealous, aren't you?'

'No!' said Min.

'You are.'

'Not!' said Min.

'Are too,' said Keith. 'My genius sister is jealous of her silly brother.'

'You don't understand,' said Min. 'How could you? You show up having done no work and everyone thinks you're amazing. But I have to work and win. Always. The more I win, the more Mum and Dad want me to win, and the more I have to work. You don't get any of that pressure.'

'I don't get any of anything,' said Keith. 'I hardly see them. They're always taking you to competitions.'

'I have to do ballet and fencing and archery, maths and physics lessons, and then there's study after dinner each evening, then competitions at the weekends and more study and …'

'Calm down, Min,' said Keith.

'… piano exams and flute exams and always trying to get the best grade and …'

Min was gulping for air. Keith knew he had to do something. He rushed into his room, grabbed his bottle of Musk Oxygen, and then waved it under Min's nose.

One whiff, and Min snapped out of her panicked state.

'That stinks,' she said.

'You stink,' said Keith.

'No, you do,' said Min.

The two of them flopped on to the bed.

'I wish I could have fun, like you,' sighed Min. 'You have time to see friends and Keith Senior and do your experiments. I never get to do anything like that. You know the most fun I had recently? When we were breathing in those helium balloons.'

'Wow,' said Keith. 'I mean, that was fun, but I have that kind of fun most days of my life.'

'I'm so worried about *Junior Mega Brain*. Mum and Dad say I have to win, as it's the last year I can compete. I'll be too old next year – under-fourteens only. If I don't win, they will send me to the horrible Hothouse Academy for the rest of the summer holiday, for more and more study, and I'll get no break at all … '

'That sounds bad,' said Keith.

'And Patterson Patterson is in the final.'

'Mr Fancy Hair and Shark Eyes?' said Keith.

'Since he moved here from America, he's been winning *everything*! He's a machine. They call him the human calculator and the super brain.'

'He's very tall,' said Keith.

'Never mind his height. He's a quizzing robot!' shouted Min.

'His initials are PP. I can't take anyone seriously called pee-pee.'

'Well, I have to take him seriously,' said Min. 'If I'm going to beat him I have to do extra hours of study, on top of my already extra hours of study … '

'Or … ' said Keith.

'Or what?' asked Min.

'Or you could just not.'

'Not what?' said Min, sitting up.

'You could just *not* study. Take a break. You're tired. And besides, you'll probably be fine. Like you just said, I showed up on the quiz without studying. Turned out OK for me. I've got fans *and* prize money.'

Min laughed slightly hysterically for a while. Keith stared calmly at her.

'Oh wow, you're serious, aren't you?' she said. 'Be more Keith, you mean?'

'Exactly!' said Keith. 'Tempted?'

'But if I lose, Mum and Dad will go nuts.'

'So?' said Keith. 'They'll get over it.'

'I'll get sent to the Hothouse Academy.'

'So?' said Keith again. 'You'd survive. I'd come and visit you. I would make you a new perfume and bring you some special flapjacks, without the varnish this time, I promise.'

Min lay back on the bed again, thinking.

'Listen, Min, do you even want to win? Do you even like quizzing? Because if you don't, I have an idea. I can't help you win the quiz, but I can help you feel OK about losing. It's not the worst thing in the world. Plus, we'll definitely have a lot of fun along the way. What do you reckon?'

Min was still thinking when she and Keith noticed blue lights strobing across the bedroom wall.

'Holy mash, Dad actually *did* call the police,' Keith said, peering out of the window.

The two of them then watched as a couple of police officers were mobbed by Keith's fans, handed sneezing rabbits, shown The Milkman's amazing milk-drinking act and persuaded to have a little dance, too.

'This is brilliant. This is so funny,' said Min, giggling. 'I've never seen a police officer dance before.'

'This is the kind of fun you can have if you stick with me, sis,' said Keith.

'OK, I'm convinced,' said Min. 'I'm in. I want to be more Keith. Now. Today. Where do we start?'

CHAPTER TWENTY-TWO

'The first thing we need to do is take a nap,' said Keith.

'Do what?' said Min. 'I never take naps.'

'You do now. It's the Keith way!' said Keith. 'Some of my best inventions have come to me while napping, but only for twenty-three minutes. I'll set a timer.'

After twenty-three minutes, Min and Keith woke up.

'That was nice,' said Min. 'I feel quite refreshed.'

'That's just the start,' said Keith. 'Now, come and see my experiments.'

Keith showed Min the toenail experiment. Still no change. He made a note in his book of Extremely Important Experiments & Inventions.

'They will never grow,' said Min. 'Nails are already dead once you can see them on your fingers, which is why it doesn't hurt to cut them.'

'Hang on, sis, I'm meant to be teaching you,' said Keith. 'What about a plant? Can that grow in a sausage?'

'Not sure,' said Min.

'Good!' said Keith. 'See, you can't learn all this stuff in books. You need to get hands-on. This is also the Keith way.'

Keith wrote Get hands-on in THE BOOK OF KEITH and then the two of them spent an hour or so before bedtime on their new experiment. They snuck outside into the back garden without their parents noticing – 'I feel like a spy,' said Min, giggling – and picked some twigs and plants. Then Min stole a fresh sausage from the fridge – 'I feel like a thief,' she said, giggling again – and they poked the greenery into the sausage, with Keith carefully noting down details. Satisfied that the experiment was successfully under way, the two of them went to bed.

The next morning, Keith was up early. When Min came down to breakfast in her pyjamas, she was surprised to see him.

'It's not eight o'clock yet,' she said. 'What are you doing here?'

'It's time for some personal styling,' said Keith.

'I know I said I wanted to be more Keith, but I don't actually want to look like you,' Min protested.

'Don't worry. We just need to connect you with the true, fun Min who is hiding behind the sensible genius exterior. To start with, I'm going to cut your hair.'

'But it has to be long for ballet, so I can put it in a bun.'

'I'll put you in a bun if you don't sit down,' Keith said. 'Now, keep very still … '

Keith sliced through Min's ponytail and began snipping her hair into a stylish bob.

'I'm a good hairdresser,' said Keith. 'I used to practise on Tom's guinea pigs. Right, what do you reckon?'

Min looked in the mirror and smiled.

'It's different,' she said. 'My hair feels lighter. I feel lighter.'

'This is just the start,' said Keith. 'I've seen what all the genius quizzers wear, you included. It's a bit dull. A lot of cardigans. I think you are much cooler, Min.'

Keith whipped out the black polo neck and massive sunglasses.

'Try this. Didn't work for me, but I think it's the perfect look for you, Min,' he said. 'And before you ask, yes, I do have an outfit for myself sorted, for the final. I reread some of my favourite books on battles and ancient warriors, for inspiration. I have an idea for a really strong look. There will be make-up, too. Quite a lot of it. Now, eat your breakfast. Then eat your breakfast again. That's another solid Keith tip. Double breakfast.'

Keith quickly wrote Geniuses eat two break-fasts in THE BOOK OF KEITH. As Min munched her way through a second portion of toast, she kept glancing at the clock.

'I feel like I should be studying,' she said. 'It's already nine thirty and I haven't done a thing.'

'You haven't done any of *your* sort of studying, but you're learning a new way from the master. That's me, by the way. Loosen up. Take your time. And finish your toast, too. Then report to my room in ten minutes. I've prepared a little quiz for you.'

Up in his room, Keith moved his desk away from the wall and sat behind it. He had jotted down some questions on cards and, when Min came in, he made her sit down in front of him.

'Min Keithstofferson, you have sixty

seconds, starting now,' he said. 'Name a famous landmark in London.'

'Erm, Big Ben?' Min said.

'No, the correct answer is Buckingham Palace,' Keith said. 'What's the record for the most people squeezed into a photo booth?'

'What? How would I know? Five?'

'Incorrect, it's seven,' said Keith.

Min snorted like an angry bull.

'What time should you go to the dentist?' Keith asked.

'Early in the morning?' Min guessed.

'Wrong, at tooth hurty!' Keith roared. 'Geddit? Two thirty. Tooth hurty!'

Min shot out of her chair.

'That's the stupidest quiz I've ever done,' she said. 'How was I supposed to get those answers right?'

'You weren't,' said Keith. 'That's the point.

I want you to see what it feels like to get questions wrong. You're learning that it's OK to lose. Don't fight it, Min. This is the new you, not some performing robot trying to please Mum and Dad.'

Min sat back down.

'Next question. Who said, "We are not amused"?'

'Queen Victoria,' said Min.

'No, it was me, just then,' said Keith. 'Name a motorway in England.'

'The M25,' said Min.

'No, the correct answer is the M6,' said Keith.

Min sighed and frowned.

'Complete this line from a famous song by the Beatles: "All you need is ..."'

'Love!' shouted Min.

'Crumpets,' said Keith. 'It was "All you

need is crumpets", they later changed it to "love".'

Min shook her head, but she was smiling a bit, too.

'How can you tell if a cow is nervous?'

'It snorts? Or stamps its feet?' Min said.

'Wrong, it mooo-ves out of the way,' said Keith.

Min laughed.

'Get the idea now?'

She nodded.

'So, when Robert Bobbinson starts firing questions at you tomorrow, what are you going to do?' Keith asked.

'Try to answer them correctly?' Min said.

'And if you don't get them right?' Keith asked.

'I'm not going to worry, too much,' muttered Min.

'Good!' said Keith. 'And if you want to be really brave, and really do things my way, what are you going to do?'

'Answer them *incorrectly*?' said Min.

'And will that be terrible, or might it actually be a tiny bit fun?'

'It might actually be a tiny bit fun,' said Min.

'Excellent!' said Keith. 'That took longer than sixty seconds, but congratulations, Min, you're beginning to Be More Keith.'

CHAPTER
TWENTY-THREE

After doing Keith's quiz, Min left some
Chinese opera playing in her room, to fool
her parents that she was in there, studying
hard for the *Junior Mega Brain* final, then
she and Keith picked their way through the
fans outside. They were excited by Min's new
haircut and crowded round her, muttering
'Sister of Keith' and stroking her hair
approvingly.

'See, my fans are your fans,' said Keith.

At the park, Keith led Min to the fish pond, for another of his Extremely Important Experiments.

'I want to discover whether fish can swim backwards,' he told Min, and pulled out yet another sausage from his backpack.

'Do all your experiments involve sausages?' Min asked.

Keith thought about it for a second.

'The majority, yes,' he said.

He attached some string to a sausage chunk, dropped it into the pond and dragged it around. Once some goldfish were interested, he dragged it in the other direction.

'The fish just turn and follow it,' Min observed. 'They don't actually reverse.'

'Hmm, I think from this we can say that fish can't swim backwards,' Keith said.

'Success! I'll log all that later when I get home. Ah, the joy of learning, eh, Min? Feels good.'

As they walked past the cafe, Keith explained how he had spat coffee over a man sitting opposite him there the other day.

'I bet I could spit coffee further,' said Min.

'You?' said Keith. 'Prove it.'

They got a cup of coffee, paying Bruce for it, and for the one Keith owed him for, then stood next to each other, took a big mouthful and spat. Keith's coffee shot forward.

'Blah, still tastes disgusting,' he said.

Then Min tried, but only managed to dribble some down her chin.

'You look like a camel eating soup,' Keith said, laughing.

Min took several more mouthfuls, which all ended up down her front or on the ground.

Keith was doubled up with laughter.

'Purse your lips more,' he said. 'Act like you really hate coffee. Come on, hate it like I hate it.'

Min took an extra-big mouthful and then, with a giant blast through her puckered-up lips, she sent coffee tearing through the air, in a big brown squirt, right into a passing runner.

'Hey, watch it!' she yelled, but Min and Keith were already off, crying with laughter as they ran.

'I have never spat coffee at a runner before,' Min gasped, laughing some more. 'It's fantastic. I can't believe what I've been missing out on, all these years.'

They ran all the way to Keith Sr's barge. He was on deck when they got there.

'Hey, both my beautiful grandkids visiting at once,' he said, hugging them. 'I can't remember the last time this happened, here, on *Drifter*. Wonderful! Let's celebrate.'

Keith Sr made a mountain of crisp sandwiches and the three of them happily tucked in, while Peanuts sat on Min's shoulder, gently nibbling her new bobbed hair. Then they all watched a few episodes of *Meet & Tuveg* and Keith explained some of the trickier backstory for Min.

Finally, as the sun began to dip and the summer evening light became mellow and golden, Keith and Min lay on the roof of *Drifter*, staring up at the sky. A cloud of tiny bugs danced high above, like they were performing just for them.

'What's two plus two?' Keith said.

'Five hundred and seventy-six,' Min said.

'What's the currency of Mongolia?'

'My trousers,' said Min.

'Good, you're getting it,' said Keith.

'I think I might take a nap,' Min said, closing her eyes and drifting off into a peaceful doze.

'I'll let you have more than twenty-three minutes,' Keith whispered. 'You've earned it.'

CHAPTER TWENTY-FOUR

Back at the house, Keith's mum and dad were in the kitchen, making dinner.

'Your hair, Min!' said Mum. 'I didn't say you could cut your hair! What possessed you?'

'You look completely different,' Dad said.

'I feel different,' said Min.

In fact, Keith thought as he looked at his sister, she seemed to be glowing. She was giving off pure Min-ness; no longer tired or stressed, but sunny and smiley and well.

This inspired Keith to work on one more new invention – the Sniffometer of Health. He knew that dogs were sometimes trained to sniff out diseases in people, so perhaps you could also sniff out wellness, too; the kind of wellness Min was radiating. They didn't have a dog, but Keith wasn't going to let that stand in his way.

Later that night, up in his room, he created a large funnel with a narrow end that fitted neatly over his nose. He sniffed his sausage experiment, which smelt meaty and just a bit mouldy, too. He sniffed his oldest teddy, Trevor, who had been under the bed for months, maybe years. Trevor smelt dusty but also familiar; a smell that made Keith feel comforted. There was no one else to try it on, though, as his family was asleep. It was late and, Keith suddenly realised, he was tired. He packed his backpack with all the things he'd need for tomorrow – the final of *Junior Mega Brain* – then he crawled into bed and fell sound asleep.

Keith woke to the sound of chanting from his fans outside. They were waving banners saying #Can'tStopTheKeith and #KeithOfCourse.

'They still seem to be chanting your name, Keith,' said Dad. 'You definitely did tell them you're not appearing in the final, didn't you?'

'Oh yeah,' said Keith. 'Did all that.'

Min appeared, in a neat cardigan.

'Looking lovely, Min,' said Dad. 'Ready for victory? Of course you are.'

Min quickly raised her eyebrows at Keith, who winked back and smiled.

Once inside the studios, Min was shown to her own private dressing room. Mum put her good luck cards up, while Dad kept banging on about winning.

'Repeat after me, Min: I live to win, I love to win. I live to win, I love to win.'

There was a knock at the door.

'Fifteen minutes until we're filming,' said the producer.

'This is it then. You can go,' said Min. 'I'm fine.'

'To win is the thing,' said Dad.

'Victory is yours,' said Mum.

'I need the loo,' said Keith.

Only, he didn't go to the loo. Once Keith was sure his parents had left the dressing room to take their seats in the audience, he returned.

'Let's go and say hi to Patterson Patterson,'

he said to Min. 'He's next door. I want to try out my new invention on him. I just want to be sure he is human. You said he was a machine, and a robot. Let's just double-check.'

Before Min could protest, Keith knocked loudly on Patterson Patterson's dressing-room door. He answered, his tall frame blocking the doorway, and stood, unsmiling, wavy hair flopping perfectly, his eyes deep and dark, like a shark's. Or perhaps a pond.

'Yes?' he said.

'Hi, I'm Keith and this is … '

'I know who you are,' said Patterson Patterson. 'The joker who disrupted my first round on the quiz. The fool with only one point, who has tricked his way on to the final.'

'Tricked?' Keith said. 'I'm back by popular demand. See, you can be wrong. Anyway, wanted to say hello, see how you are and wish you good luck.'

'Luck doesn't come into it,' said Patterson Patterson. His pond eyes narrowed. Then he noticed the huge funnel Keith was holding.

'What's that?' he asked. 'Wait! What are you doing?'

Keith raised the Sniffometer of Health, pointed it at Patterson Patterson and inhaled deeply.

'How dare you sniff me with that con-traption!'

'I was just conducting a little health check-up, nothing to stress about,' said Keith. 'Anyway, we best go. Min needs to finish getting ready. My dad says I can't compete in the quiz. That's what he says. But anyway, break a leg and all that.'

'That was pretty mad, Keith,' said Min, back in her dressing room. 'You do know he's not really a robot, he just acts like one?'

'I know, the Sniffometer got all that, but it also picked up something else. A funny smell. A sort of slightly sweaty, grown-up smell, like how Dad smells when he's been vacuuming the stairs. Interesting.'

Min bundled Keith outside to wait while she got changed. She appeared a few moments later. The cardigan was gone. The polo neck was on. She was dressed all in black.

'You look awesome,' said Keith.

He gave her a hug.

'Hey, mind the sunglasses,' Min laughed.

'Now remember everything I taught you,' said Keith. 'Don't worry about how you do or what Mum and Dad think, just enjoy yourself. It's going to be great. You're going to be great. And I'm right behind you. Trust me!'

'OK, I can do this.' Min smiled. 'I can Be More Keith.'

'Right on. That's all you have to do,' he said. 'Be More Keith.'

CHAPTER
TWENTY-FIVE

Out in the studio audience, Keith and Min's parents were sitting and waiting. Keith Sr was there, too, his purple cape on, Peanuts perched on his shoulder, with Keith's best friend, Tom, next to him. All Keith's biggest fans, the ones who had been camped out in his front garden for days, were dotted about – Big Puffy, the ex-wrestler; The Milkman; the Scottish family with all eight Chilean sneezing rabbits. Beyond, there were hundreds of other excited fans, all chanting 'Can't stop the Keith!'

'Keith told his fans he's not going to appear,' said Keith's dad. 'Why are they shouting for him?'

'And where is he?' said his mum.

There was no time to find him. The lights dipped and a voice boomed through the studio.

'Ladies, gentlemen and children. Welcome to the final of *Junior Mega Brain*!'

The theme music played and the audience clapped madly. The mood was more rock concert than child-genius quiz. The voiceover boomed again.

'Please welcome your host, Robert Bobbinson.'

Robert Bobbinson strode out on to the

stage in a sharp grey suit, his face as serious as a stone, and took his place at the quiz-master's desk.

'Now, let's bring on our finalists,' he said. 'Patterson Patterson and Minerva Keithstofferson.'

The two young geniuses walked out to applause. Patterson Patterson was wearing his leather jacket and dark jeans, and, walking behind, was Min.

'What on earth is she wearing?' Mum exclaimed.

Min's all-black outfit looked super sharp, her sleek bobbed hair gleamed in the studio lights, and her eyes were hidden behind giant sunglasses.

'Finally, back by popular demand and competing on a wild card, please welcome Keith Keithstofferson!'

The audience shot to its feet, cheering, whistling and whooping. The spotlight searched the stage, the music blared, the Chilean sneezing rabbits sneezed – but where was Keith? People began muttering 'Where is he?' Then the mutters became a chant, a single chant, rising in volume, until everyone was shouting.

'Keith! Keith! Keith! Keith!'

The studio seemed to shake. Patterson Patterson glowered. Min grinned.

Still no sign of Keith.

'Perhaps Keith has decided not to compete,' said Robert Bobbinson.

'I told him not to,' shouted Keith's dad, standing up. 'I didn't want him to make a fool of himself.'

The audience booed. Someone shouted 'Meany'. Then some others repeated their chants of 'Keith!' until Robert Bobbinson raised his hand.

'In that case, we will continue,' he said. 'Let's have silence, please, so we can begin the first round.'

He picked up the question cards and …

'Not so fast, Robbo!' came a voice.

The audience gasped. The spotlight spun to the back. A boy was standing there, with spiked-up hair, a furry jacket, tartan trousers and, amazingly, a completely blue face.

'I believe I have some genius quizzing to do.'

'Keith!' roared the audience.

Everyone leaped to their feet, cheering and clapping.

'He's blue,' Keith's mum whimpered. 'Why is he blue?'

Keith walked slowly through the audience, fist-bumping his fans, bowing and waving,

until he finally took his seat onstage next to Min.

'You look amazing,' she whispered to him.

Not everyone agreed.

'You shouldn't let him compete, looking like that,' said Patterson Patterson. 'His face is blue. That must be against quiz guidelines.'

'I've gone for the Celtic warrior look,' said Keith. 'They painted themselves with blue woad before battle. I think it brings out my eyes.'

Patterson Patterson snorted.

Robert Bobbinson raised his hand again. The audience went quiet.

'Unfortunately, there are no specific rules about dress,' he said. 'I have no choice but to say: Let the final of the *Junior Mega Brain* quiz begin.'

CHAPTER TWENTY-SIX

The first round was maths. Patterson Patterson had his turn and romped through the questions, answering like a robot, quickly and accurately. He scored nine points.

Min was up next. Keith's fans yelled, 'Sister of Keith, Sister of Keith.' Keith couldn't see her expression behind her sunglasses, but her shoulders looked tense.

Robert Bobbinson began firing questions

and Min, through pure habit, began answering them correctly. She only got one wrong, and scored eight points.

'What was that?' Keith whispered, as his sister sat down next to him.

'I'm sorry, I panicked. I'm so used to answering questions right.'

'You're supposed to be getting stuff wrong, losing, having fun,' he said.

Then he whipped out his Sniffometer of Health and inhaled Min deeply.

'You smell all sour and tense now,' said Keith. 'Not good, Min. Remember your training! Be More Keith.'

Min nodded quickly.

Next, it was Keith's go.

'Your minute starts now,' said Robert Bobbinson. 'What's thirty-three multiplied six times, divided by three squared?'

'Is it sixty-four?' said Keith.

It wasn't. The audience cheered.

'Why are they cheering when he's got it wrong?' asked Keith's dad. 'This makes no sense at all.'

'What's minus five times minus five, subtract twelve, add forty-three?'

'Is it sixty-four?' said Keith.

It wasn't. The audience cheered again.

For every question, Keith answered 'Is it sixty-four?' and by the final question, the entire audience shouted 'Is it sixty-four?' before collapsing into laughter.

'Keith Keithstofferson, you have a total of zero points,' said Robert Bobbinson at the end of the round.

The audience roared and yelled, 'We love you, Keith!'

'No one is taking this seriously,' Keith's

dad muttered. Keith's mum was frowning and shaking her head.

'At the end of the first round, Patterson Patterson is in the lead,' said Robert Bobbinson.

'This would be a good time to get out my mascot, I think,' said Keith. He rummaged in his backpack and then plonked the sausage with the toenails stuck in it on the desk.

'That's completely disgusting,' said Patterson Patterson, holding his nose.

'It's actually one of my Extremely Important Experiments,' said Keith.

'Let's continue,' said Robert Bobbinson.

'Hold up, Robbo, you're rushing again,' said Keith. 'I was just going to have a little snack. Thinking makes me hungry.'

Keith produced a bowl from under his desk.

'I made this by waterproofing old bread with varnish,' he said.

There was an 'Oohh' and some light applause from the audience.

He poured in cereal, splashed on some milk, then whipped out something that looked like a cross between a comb and a spoon.

'This is my sucking fork,' said Keith. 'Another of my inventions. Perfect for eating mushy food. Do you want a go, PP?'

'Have a go, PP!' someone shouted.

'Yeah, try the sucking fork, PP,' someone else shouted.

'My name is Patterson Patterson,' he fumed.

'Pat-a-cake, Pat-a-cake?' Keith said.

The audience giggled.

'Enough! Let's get on with the quiz,' said Robert Bobbinson.

'Sure thing, Bob,' said Keith. 'As soon as I get my brain cooler on.'

Keith rummaged below the desk again and pulled out Keith's Anti-Heat Headgear, which was a headband with two stiff wires attached, each with a small fan at the end. Keith pulled it on to his head, switched on the fans and began wiggling the wires.

'Let me help you,' said Keith Sr, striding down to Keith and adjusting the headset.

'Thanks,' said Keith. 'You can't think straight when your brain's hot. I found that out when I did a maths test with a woolly hat on.'

'Clear the studio floor,' said Robert Bobbinson.

Keith Sr headed back to his seat, with Peanuts flying low over the contestants squawking 'Cheesy chips, cheesy chips'.

By now, Patterson Patterson was fidgeting and shaking his head.

'This is ridiculous,' he said. 'Is anybody actually in charge here?'

'Relax, PP,' said Keith. 'This is supposed to be fun. We're all having a good time, why aren't you?'

'I know what you're up to, Keithstofferson.

You're trying to put me off with your stupid sausage toenails and blue face paint. It won't work. Nothing stands in the way of Patterson Patterson.'

At that exact moment, Peanuts flew past and dropped a tiny white splat on to his expensive leather jacket.

'Oooh, look, PP,' said Keith. 'That's good luck.'

CHAPTER
TWENTY-SEVEN

The next round was about the meaning of words. Min stepped up to the podium and took off her sunglasses.

'I'm ready,' she said.

By 'ready', she meant ready to answer 'bibble' and 'diddynope' and 'grittens' to every single question. She got zero points. The audience were shocked into silence at first, then began to understand what was happening, and a wave of joy spread through the studio, with chants of 'Sister of Keith' and loud cheering.

'What is she doing? *What is she doing?*' Min's dad gasped.

Min's mum shot up from her chair and shouted out: 'Min, this is not how geniuses behave. Think about what you're doing. You are throwing away victory. I don't understand. To win is the thing!'

Min simply put her sunglasses back on and returned to her seat. Patterson Patterson barged past her.

'My go, let's get on with this,' he said.

'Chill out, Patterson,' someone shouted.

'Keep It Keith,' someone else shouted.

'Question one,' said Robert Bobbinson. 'What ten-letter word starting with the letter L describes someone who is sad and gloomy?'

'Leaking!' someone shouted from the audience. 'Your bowl's leaking, Keith.'

It was The Milkman. He was right. Keith's bread bowl was not as waterproofed as he had hoped. The milk was dripping on to the studio floor.

'Let me help,' said The Milkman. 'I've had a lot of experience with spilt milk.'

Lured by the little chunks of soggy bread and cereal that were splatting down, the rabbits hopped after him, sneezing excitedly.

'Holy moly,' shouted Keith Sr. 'It's a rabbit stampede!'

The audience whooped. Who doesn't like a rabbit stampede? Patterson Patterson, that's who. He went pale.

'I hate rabbits,' he muttered, climbing on to the desk. 'Are they sick? Why are they sneezing? I can't afford to get ill. This

is ridiculous. I can't carry on in these con-
ditions.'

'You don't look too well,' said Keith. 'Let
me examine you.'

Keith whipped out the Sniffometer of
Health from below the desk and took a big
whiff of Patterson Patterson again.

'Same as earlier,' said Keith. 'A sort of
unwell grown-up smell. It's that sweaty
adult whiff again. Doesn't seem like the
right smell for someone competing in *Junior
Mega Brain*. You are under fourteen, aren't
you, PP?'

'What are you saying?' Patterson Patterson
asked.

'I'm asking, are you under fourteen years
old?' Keith said.

Patterson Patterson began breathing hard.

'Come on, PP, you're normally really quick

at answering questions,' said Keith. 'I'll ask it one more time: are you under fourteen?'

'Keith Keithstofferson, that's enough,' said Robert Bobbinson. 'Be quiet.'

'Nope,' said Keith. 'I won't be quiet. Not right now.'

He jumped up on to the desk next to Patterson Patterson and stared him right in the face.

'I've always thought there was something funny going on with you, PP, and now, with the help of my Sniffometer of Health, I've figured it out.'

Keith turned to the audience.

'Everybody! I believe that Patterson Patterson here is at least sixteen. His smell gives him away. And just look how tall he is. That means only one thing. Patterson Patterson is appearing illegally because this quiz is for *under-fourteens only.*'

The audience gasped.

'Rubbish!' Patterson Patterson shouted, staring into Keith's blue face with his black, pondy-shark eyes. 'Where's your proof?'

'The Sniffometer of Health doesn't lie,' said Keith.

'That's not proper evidence.'

'Proper enough,' said Keith.

'Patterson Patterson, are you over

fourteen years old?' Robert Bobbinson asked, looking stern enough to crack glass. 'Is Keith correct? You can put these silly accusations to bed right now. Simply tell us the truth.'

The studio fell silent. All eyes were on Patterson Patterson. He swallowed hard, glanced around nervously and seemed about to speak, but instead, before anyone could stop him, he jumped clean off the desk and ran.

'Seal the area!' Keith roared. 'Now! We've got a bolter.'

CHAPTER
TWENTY-EIGHT

Patterson Patterson ran towards the doors at the back of the studio, but some of Keith's fans jumped up and slammed them shut, before he could escape. Patterson Patterson then swerved into the audience, leaping across the seat backs. Halfway along he toppled to the floor, and there were cries of 'Catch him, catch him!' but he wriggled clear of the grabbing hands and zoomed back on to the studio floor – where he screeched to a halt. His path was blocked by all eight Chilean sneezing rabbits, in a line in front of him.

ATISHOO!

The rabbits sneezed at exactly the same time, right at him.

'I hate rabbits!' PP screamed, dashing off again.

'Don't let him escape,' Keith yelled, lobbing his sucking fork at him, but just missing. Min grabbed at his leather jacket, but PP slipped it off and carried on running.

'Stop him, he's getting away,' she yelled.

Keith reached into his backpack and pulled out … a pot of Marmite.

'Open the doors,' he yelled.

'But PP might escape,' shouted Min.

'Do as I say,' Keith shouted. The doors were shoved open.

Then Keith stuck two fingers in his mouth and whistled.

Nothing happened for one second, two seconds, then, pouring through the doors came a great grey cloud. It was pigeons, lots of them. Eager for a Marmite treat, and ready to help the genius boy who held their favourite spread.

'Get him!' Keith yelled, pointing at PP, dodging around the studio.

The pigeons swooped down on Patterson Patterson, pecking his perfect hair. He flapped his arms madly, trying to shoo them away.

'Milkman, use your milk!' Keith shouted. 'Big Puffy, do your wrestling moves!'

The Milkman rushed forward and emptied some oat milk on to the floor just ahead of PP, who ran straight into it. He began skidding and slipping and then:

WHAM!

Big Puffy hurled himself through the air, tackled PP to the floor and sat on him.

'Sweet!' said Keith.

'Amazing!' said Min.

'Hoorah!' roared the audience.

'Get off me,' Patterson Patterson panted. 'I'm a genius.'

'The only thing you are, mate, is busted,' said Big Puffy.

A crowd gathered on the studio floor. Eventually, Big Puffy got off and let Patterson Patterson stand up. He was a sorry sight, his perfect hair messed up, his white T-shirt stained.

'Do you have anything to say for yourself?' Robert Bobbinson asked.

He shook his head.

'Why did you do it?' Keith asked. 'Come

on, we all deserve an answer.'

'I wanted to win,' Patterson Patterson replied. 'I didn't want to give up genius quizzing, just because I'm sixteen. What would I do if I wasn't winning?'

'You could go to the park or watch *Meet & Tuveg*. Or do Extremely Important Experiments and Inventions. There's tons you can do. Winning isn't everything. Here, why don't you try on my Anti-Heat Headgear?' Keith said, taking it off and passing it to Patterson Patterson.

'I could come round to yours and show you how to make genius kit like this, if you like. I mean, yeah, you're pretty annoying, but that's OK. You just need to Be More Keith.'

Patterson Patterson was led away, but he looked back over his shoulder at Keith, and gave him a tiny nod. Keith nodded back.

'I'll join you, too, when you're making genius kit and going to the park,' said Min. 'That's what I want to do more of, from now on.'

'What are you saying, Min?' Mum asked.

'I want some time off, to relax and just be myself,' she said. 'I don't want any more pressure. I don't want to study endlessly. I want to spend time with Keith, hanging out and having fun.'

'But you're a child genius,' Dad protested.

'Well, I'd like to lose the genius bit and just be a child, please,' Min said. 'There's more to life than competing. You can send me to the Hothouse Academy if you want, for losing here, I don't care. But after that, I'm having a new life.'

'Or you could spend the money that it would cost to send Min to the Hothouse

Academy on a holiday for all four of us, as a family,' said Keith. 'What do you think?'

Min and Keith's parents looked stunned.

'Give them a minute to think it all through,' Keith Sr said, steering Min and Keith away. 'Hey, Robert Bobbinson, now that Patterson Patterson is disqualified, who are you going to give that big old trophy to? I'd say my grandkids are worthy winners, wouldn't you, for services to truth, creativity and good times.'

Robert Bobbinson thought for a second, then picked up the huge shiny trophy and passed it to Keith with a stern nod. Keith took the trophy and gazed at it for a moment, his blue face reflected back at him in its golden surface. Then he turned to the audience, held the trophy high above his head and let out a mighty roar.

CHAPTER TWENTY-NINE

For the next two hours, the TV studios where the *Junior Mega Brain* final should have been taking place became a full-on party. The Milkman did his act and one of the producers promised to get him on to a variety show. Keith Sr was dancing with Keith's fans to 'The Keith Is On' with a rabbit on each shoulder, and Big Puffy the ex-wrestler had pigeons perched all over him and was feeding them Marmite.

Min grabbed the mouldy sausage with toenails sticking out of it and chased people around the studio with it, shrieking with laughter.

'Look, I'm having actual fun!' she yelled.

Then she lobbed the sausage towards Keith and it got impaled on his spiky hair, like a marshmallow on a hedgehog.

It was a while before Keith looked up to see his mum and dad gazing at him from their seats. They were smiling. Not the full grin he'd seen in photos of Min winning prizes, but still a smile.

He squeezed through the crowds to reach them.

'We're just trying to take it all in,' said his mum, picking the sausage out of his hair. 'Maybe we have pushed Min too hard and maybe we have overlooked you. All those amazing experiments. We had no idea. And you were able to work out that Patterson Patterson was an imposter, too, with your sniffing-cone thingy.'

'Sniffometer of Health,' said Keith.

'Yes, that,' said his mum. 'It's amazing. We are proud of you.'

'Really?' said Keith.

'Yes, very proud of you, son,' said his dad. 'We realise now that there's more than one kind of genius. You may not be like Min, but you're a genius all the same.'

Then he ruffled Keith's hair. Or tried to.

'Ouch, that really is spiky. What did you use on that?'

'Varnish,' said Keith. 'It's so versatile.'

Min whizzed past, shouting 'You'll never take me alive', followed by eight rabbits. Then she tripped and fell over and the rabbits piled on top, nuzzling her excitedly.

'First a rabbit stampede, then a rabbit pile-up,' said Keith Sr, joining the others. 'Good times.'

Keith hugged his grandad and his parents, with Peanuts squawking 'Camembert' noisily. The party bounced on for some time, until eventually the studio manager said everyone had to leave so they could clean up and start filming a cookery show.

On the way home, Keith sighed happily.

'That was the best fun ever,' he said. 'And we even won. Just look at that trophy. It's a beauty.'

'Does that mean I don't have to go to the Hothouse Academy?' Min asked.

'Sure, take the rest of the summer off,' said Dad.

'Your hair's too short for ballet anyway,' said Mum. 'You and Keith can spend some time together. Maybe you'd like to go to the Inventors' Fair together? Or maybe we could all go? What do you think?'

'Yes, yes, yes!' said Keith, 'I'd love you to come, all of you. And I'm paying for it with my prize money, remember?'

'That's fantastic, Keith. Then afterwards we'll travel around France for a bit, have a holiday,' said Keith's dad.

'This is going to be amazing. The fair is going to blow your minds. So many amazing inventions to see. I might take my sucking fork along, see what all the genius inventors think of it.'

Then he wound down the window and shouted out, to no one in particular: 'I'm going to the Inventors' Fair! Waaahhh!'

Everyone laughed.

'I'd also like to watch that detective show you like so much, Keith,' his mum said. 'What's it called? *Mince & Toomuch*?'

Everyone laughed again.

It was the first time all four of them had laughed together for a very long time. It wasn't until the car turned on to their street that the laughing stopped. Hundreds of fans were milling around outside the house. Some of them had painted their faces blue like Keith's.

'Not this again!' sighed Keith's dad. 'Look, I do really, finally realise that you're incredibly talented, Keith, and a great inventor, but I can't put up with these fans on our doorstep. You have to make them go.'

Min and Keith got out of the car. The fans raced towards them. They wanted photos. They especially wanted THE BOOK OF KEITH.

'We need to read your genius wisdom, Keith,' they said. 'When can we read it?'

'What shall I do, Min?' Keith said, once inside. 'They're waiting for THE BOOK OF KEITH and it's not finished yet.'

'It's obvious, isn't it?' said Min. 'Thought you were supposed to be a genius.'

She ran upstairs to Keith's room and came back down with a bottle of brown liquid.

'If that doesn't get rid of them, I don't know what will,' said Min.

'Musk Oxygen: The Smell of a Genius. Of course,' said Keith. 'Thanks, Min.'

'No, thank you, Keith,' said Min, and she hugged him quickly before opening the front door.

'Now, get out there and release the stink.'

Keith grinned, grabbed the bottle and stepped outside.

BORED OF YOUR BROTHER?

SICK OF YOUR SISTER?

READY FOR A BRAND NEW, SUPERCOOL SIBLING?

READ ON FOR AN EXTRACT FROM THIS LAUGH-OUT-LOUD ADVENTURE FROM

JO SIMMONS

CHAPTER ONE

CLICK!

CHANGE BROTHERS AND SWITCH SISTERS
TODAY WITH
www.siblingswap.com

The advert popped up in the corner of the screen. Jonny clicked on it instantly. The Sibling Swap website pinged open, showing smiling brothers and happy sisters, all playing and laughing and having a great time together.

What crazy alternative universe was this? Where were the big brothers teasing their little brothers about being rubbish at climbing and slow at everything? Where were the wedgies and ear flicks? What about the name-calling? This looked like a world

Jonny had never experienced, a world in which brothers and sisters actually *liked* each other!

'Oh sweet mangoes of heaven!' Jonny muttered.

It was pretty bonkers, but it was definitely tempting. No, scrap that: it was *essential*. Jonny couldn't believe his luck. Just think what Sibling Swap could offer him.

A new brother. A *better* brother. A brother who didn't put salt in his orange squash, who didn't call him a human sloth, who didn't burp in his ear. That kind of brother.

Jonny had to try it. He could always return the new brother if things didn't work out. It was a no-brainer.

He clicked on the application form.

What could go wrong?

CHAPTER TWO

FIGHT, FATE, FORMS

Only a little while before Jonny saw the Sibling Swap advert, he and his older brother, Ted, had had a fight. Another fight.

It was a particularly stupid fight, and it had started like all stupid fights do – over something stupid. This time, pants. But not just any pants. The Hanging Pants of Doom.

Jonny and Ted were walking their dog, Widget, on the nearby Common. They arrived at a patch of woodland, where an exceptionally large and colourful pair of men's pants had been hanging in a tree for ages. These pants had become legendary over the years the brothers had been playing here. There was a horrible glamour about them. The boys were grossed out and slightly scared of them, but could never quite ignore them. And so the pants had become the Hanging Pants of Doom, and now, unfortunately, Jonny had just lobbed Widget's Frisbee into the tree. It was stuck in a branch, just below the mythical underwear.

'Oh swear word,' said Jonny.

'Nice one!' said Ted. 'You threw it up there, so you have to get it down.'

Jonny frowned. Two problems presented themselves. One was the fact that the Frisbee was very close to the pants, making the possibility of touching the revolting garment very real. Second, Jonny wasn't very good at climbing.

'Go on, Jonny, up you go,' teased Ted. 'Widget can't wait all day for his Frisbee. Climb up and get it ... What's that? You're rubbish at climbing? Sorry, what? You would prefer it if I went and got the Frisbee, as I'm truly excellent at climbing?'

'All RIGHT!' fumed Jonny, ripping off his jacket. 'I'll climb up and get it. Look after my coat.'

'Thanks!' said Ted. 'I might use it as a blanket. You're so slow, we could be here until midnight.'

Jonny began his climb slowly, as Ted had predicted, and rather shakily, as Ted had also predicted.

'I'm just taking my time, going carefully. Don't rush me!' said Jonny, as he reached for the next branch.

'Spare us the running commentary,' Ted said.

After several minutes, a tiny dog appeared below the tree, followed by its elderly owner, and it began yapping up at Jonny.

'That's my brother up there,' Ted said to the

lady, pointing up. 'He's thrown his pants into the tree again and has to go and get them.'

The lady squinted up. Her dog continued yip-yapping.

'Oh yes, I see,' she said. 'Well, they're rather splendid pants, aren't they? I can see why he wants to get them back. Are those spaceships on them?'

'Cars,' said Ted.

'Very fetching,' said the lady. 'But he shouldn't throw them into the trees again. A magpie might get them.'

'That's what I told him,' said Ted, trying not to laugh. 'Sorry, I better go and help or we'll be here until Christmas. He's like a human sloth!'

With that, Ted bounced up into the tree, pulling himself quickly up its branches and passing his brother, just as Jonny was within touching distance of the Frisbee.

'Got it!' said Ted, snatching the Frisbee and tossing it down to Widget, before swinging off a branch and landing neatly on his feet. 'You can come down now, bro. Unless you really do want to touch the Pants of Doom. You're pretty close, actually. Look! They're just there.'

Jonny made a noise in his throat – a bit like a growl – and felt his face burning bright red. He was shaking with anger and humiliation as he slowly began making his way down.

By the time the brothers banged back into the house, Jonny was speechless with fury. He ran upstairs. He could hear his mum telling him off for slamming the front door, but too bad. He smashed his bedroom door shut too. There! How's that? He was sick of Ted teasing him, sick of being the younger brother. And as for telling that old lady that the Hanging Pants of Doom were *his* ...

Jonny flipped open his laptop and, miraculously, there was the Sibling Swap website telling him that all this could change. What perfect timing. Had the Sibling Swap team climbed into his head and read his thoughts? Who cared?

He read the home page:

SOMETIMES YOU DON'T GET THE BROTHER OR SISTER YOU DESERVE, BUT HERE AT SIBLING SWAP, WE AIM TO PUT THAT RIGHT. WITH SO MANY BROTHERS AND SISTERS OUT THERE, WE CAN MATCH YOU TO THE PERFECT ONE!

His heart began to beat faster.

SWAPPING YOUR BROTHER OR SISTER HAS NEVER BEEN EASIER WITH SIBLING SWAP! SIMPLY FILL OUT THE APPLICATION FORM

AND WE WILL SUPPLY YOU WITH A NEW BROTHER OR SISTER WITHIN TWENTY-FOUR HOURS, CAREFULLY CHOSEN FROM OUR MASSIVE DATABASE OF POSSIBLE MATCHES. OUR DEDICATED TEAM OF SWAP OPERATIVES WORKS 24/7 TO FIND THE BEST MATCH FOR YOU, BUT IF YOU ARE NOT COMPLETELY HAPPY, YOU CAN RETURN YOUR REPLACEMENT SIBLING FOR A NEW MATCH OR YOUR ORIGINAL BROTHER OR SISTER.

Amazing! For the first time in his almost ten years, this website was offering Jonny power, choice, freedom! It felt good! He rubbed his hands together and began filling out the form.

First, there were two options:

ARE YOU SWAPPING A SIBLING?

ARE YOU PUTTING YOURSELF UP TO BE SWAPPED?

'Easy,' Jonny muttered. 'I'm the one doing the swapping. Me. I have the power!' He did a sort of evil genius laugh as he clicked on the top box. By Tic Tacs, this was exciting! Next, the form asked:

ARE YOU SWAPPING A BROTHER OR SISTER?

'Also easy,' muttered Jonny. 'Brother.'

Then:

WOULD YOU LIKE TO RECEIVE A BROTHER OR A SISTER?

Jonny clicked the box marked 'Brother'. Then he had to add some information about himself.

AGE: NINE.

HOBBIES: BIKING, SWIMMING, COMPUTER GAMES, DOUGHNUTS, MESSING ABOUT.

LEAST FAVOURITE THINGS:

- **MY BROTHER, TED (HE TEASES ME ALL**

THE TIME AND RECKONS HE'S COOL JUST BECAUSE HE GOES TO SECONDARY SCHOOL)

- **BEING NINE (I *AM* NEARLY TEN, BUT CAN I HAVE A BROTHER WHO IS YOUNGER THAN ME OR MAYBE THE SAME AGE PLEASE?)**
- **SPROUTS**
- **CLIMBING**
- **BEING SICK**

Then there was a whole page about the kind of brother Jonny might like. He quickly ticked the following boxes: fun; adventurous; enjoys food; enjoys sports and swimming; likes dogs. He didn't tick the box marked 'living' or the one marked 'human'. He just wanted a brother, so it was obvious, wasn't it?

That ought to do it, Jonny reckoned. His heart was galloping now. In just three minutes it was ready to send. He sat back in his chair. 'Just one click,' he said, 'and I get a brother upgrade by this time tomorrow. Friday, in fact! Ready for the weekend!'

Jonny felt slightly dizzy. He giggled quietly to himself. He felt giddy with power! All he had to do was send off the form. Easy! But then he hesitated … Should he do this? Was it OK? Would he get into trouble? Jonny's dad no longer lived with him and Ted, so he might not notice, but what would his mum say? She'd be pleased, Jonny decided quickly. Yes! After all, she was fed up with Jonny and Ted arguing. This was the perfect solution. Then, with a tiny frown, he wondered how Ted might feel about being swapped, but before he could puzzle this out, there was his brother again, shouting up the stairs.

'Dinner, loser!' Ted yelled. 'Let me know if you need help climbing down the stairs.

They *are* quite steep. It could take you a while.'

That was it! For the second time that day, Jonny felt the anger bubbling up inside like a can of shaken Pixie Fizz. Enough! Double enough!

'So I'm the rubbish younger brother, am I? Well, here's one thing I can do really brilliantly,' he muttered and, jutting out his chin, hit the send button.

CLICK!

'Done!' he said, and slammed the laptop shut.

HEAD TO
www.siblingswap.com
TODAY
... your future sibling awaits!

Change brothers and switch sisters!

Sometimes you don't get the brother or sister you deserve, but here at Sibling Swap, we aim to put that right. With so many brothers and sisters out there, we can match you to the perfect one!

So what are you waiting for?
Get SWAPPING!

- Take the quiz to find your perfect brother or sister
- Meet the founder of Sibling Swap
- Download fun activities and games to play with (or without) your sibling!